"I Didn't Think You Could Be Attracted To Someone Like Me,"

Erin told Logan.

"What do you mean, someone like you?"

"I'm so ordinary."

He gave a snort of derision and gripped her shoulders. "You, my lady, are lovely and quite special. You possess a gentle soul and an unusual degree of honesty, which are rare qualities in this superficial society we live in. What surprises me is that some man hasn't broken through your defenses and convinced you of that before now."

"No one's ever cared enough to try."

"I care," he murmured softly, "but I'm not going to lie to you, Erin. I would be faithful to you while we're lovers, but I've never been much good at lasting relationships, and I probably never will be. Marriage is a silken trap I have no intention of being caught in. I want you more than any woman I've ever known, but I can't promise you hearts and flowers forever."

Dear Reader:

Welcome to Silhouette Desire—sensual, compelling, believable love stories written by and for today's woman. When you open the pages of a Silhouette Desire, you open yourself up to a whole new world— a world of promising passion and endless love.

Each and every Silhouette Desire is a wonderful love story that is both sensuous *and* emotional. You're with the hero and heroine each and every step of the way—from their first meeting, to their first kiss ... to their happy ending. You'll experience all the deep joys—and occasional tribulations—of falling in love.

In future months, look for Silhouette Desire novels from some of your favorite authors, such as Annette Broadrick, Dixie Browning, Kathleen Korbel and Lass Small, just to name a few.

So go wild with Desire. You'll be glad you did!

Lucia Macro
Senior Editor

NOELLE BERRY McCUE

LOOK BEYOND THE DREAM

SILHOUETTE *Desire*

Published by Silhouette Books New York

America's Publisher of Contemporary Romance

SILHOUETTE BOOKS
300 East 42nd St., New York, N.Y. 10017

Copyright © 1990 by Noelle Berry McCue

ISBN: 0-373-05572-2

First Silhouette Books printing June 1990

Printed in the U.S.A.

Books by Noelle Berry McCue

Silhouette Desire

Magic Touch #510
Look Beyond the Dream #572

**Books by Noelle Berry McCue
writing as Nicole Monet**

Silhouette Desire

Love's Silver Web #2
Shadow of Betrayal #39
Passionate Silence #62
Love and Old Lace #133
Casey's Shadow #177
Rand Emory's Woman #228
The Sandcastle Man #266
Stand by Me #405
Twilight over Eden #473

Silhouette Romance

Guardian Angel #615

NOELLE BERRY McCUE,

who helped launch the Silhouette Desire line under the pseudonym Nicole Monet, lives in California. "I've always loved to read," the author says, "and writing has filled a void in me I was never consciously aware of having. It has added depth to my life, and a greater awareness and appreciation of the people around me. With every book I write, I hope I am in some small way paying for the pleasure reading has given me over the years. If I can help just one person find enjoyment and release from everyday troubles, then I've accomplished my purpose in my chosen field."

The author concludes by saying, "That's why I write romances, because they leave the reader with a positive attitude toward love, life and relationships. When all is said and done, isn't it love for others that gives us the greatest happiness in life?"

One

Erin Daniels slid from the seat of her ancient Volkswagen bug and automatically smoothed down the gabardine skirt, which had ridden up her thighs as she drove across town. Settling the matching rust-colored jacket at her waist, she eyed her shapely legs with disfavor. She would have preferred them to be much less curved and quite a bit longer, but she only stood just under five foot four and had long ago resigned herself to her lack of stature.

Because she was short, with an oval, pink-cheeked baby face, it was a normal occurrence for most people she met to automatically treat her with amused indulgence, when what she wanted was to be taken seriously. She caught sight of her reflection in the car window, and brushed a long strand of straight, fine blond hair from her cheek with an irritated gesture.

Proving she was more than a cute face and an empty-headed body had been an uphill struggle, but she had eventually managed to graduate from both her provincial Idaho high school and the University of California at Berkeley with honors.

Linda Morelli, her best friend and dormitory roommate throughout college, was a tall, elegantly slim woman of Italian descent, whose indolent nature concealed a razor-sharp mind. Linda was outgoing and definitely a social animal, and had often decried Erin's diligent study habits. Especially when, she remembered with a smile, they had interfered with the parties and extracurricular school activities Linda had wanted Erin to attend.

But as a psychology major Linda had understood Erin's need to attain the goals she'd set for herself, and on the whole the two women had gotten along unusually well for such divergent personalities. So much so that they had rented a small apartment together after graduation, both of them working part-time as waitresses at a nearby restaurant to meet expenses while they studied for their masters' degrees.

A little over six months ago they had each passed the examinations entitling them to the much-longed-for advanced degree, and Linda had almost immediately been hired as a junior staff psychologist at a private health clinic in downtown Oakland. Erin, however, hadn't been as fortunate. She had lost count of the number of jobs she'd applied for and the disappointments suffered as a result. Since her qualifications were excellent, she'd reached the conclusion that her appearance was proving a detriment to advancement.

After all, she reflected sourly, what employer was going to believe that a woman who looked like a damn Kewpie doll was capable of handling responsibility?

Linda had seen the advertisement for a trained dietary technician in their local paper, and yesterday morning Erin had called the number given, her fingers trembling with subdued hope. It had been that of an employment agency, and after stating her qualifications she was asked to drop by their office as soon as possible. She had done so, and the woman who spoke with her had been enthusiastic enough to immediately phone and arrange an interview for her at a health club in nearby Piedmont.

Upon learning the details of the position she was applying for, some of Erin's excitement had abruptly waned. When she envisioned a health club, she imagined bodies in various shapes and sizes running around in skintight leotards. As an employee of such an establishment, she'd wondered, would she be expected to adopt the same mode of dress? There was no way in heaven or hell, she had decided with an inward shudder, that she was going to stuff herself into such a figure-revealing garment.

The mere idea was enough to make her clench her teeth in silent protest, and as she slammed her car door shut she asked herself what in the world she was doing applying for a job in such a ritzy area as this. Piedmont was an affluent neighborhood, populated for the most part by men and women with the wealth to indulge in a quest for eternal youth. Whether fashionably slim and healthy or overindulged and jaded, such worldly, sophisticated people would have little in common with a former Idaho farm girl.

Erin swallowed with difficulty, trying to ignore the nervous fluttering in her stomach as she remembered voicing her doubts to Linda upon returning to their small apartment from the employment agency. Regrettably for once her friend hadn't understood her point of view. When told the name of her potential employer, her voice had risen to an incredulous shriek. "You have an interview with Logan Sinclair? *The* Logan Sinclair?"

Frowning in puzzlement at the excitement sparkling in the depths of Linda's jet-black eyes, Erin nodded. "Why, is he somebody important?"

"He's just the only son and heir of the Berkeley Sinclairs, one of the most socially prominent families in the Bay Area. Honestly, see what you miss when you refuse to read the society columns in the newspaper? If you did, you'd have instantly recognized him by name and reputation."

Erin's eyes widened in dismay, her voice quivering slightly with apprehension. "Reputation?"

"Mmm, the man is not noted for his saintly qualities," Linda responded dreamily, "but with his looks and money he doesn't have to worry about celibacy. There was a picture of him featured at a gala fundraising affair last month, squiring that new fashion model who's all the rage at the moment."

Erin knew the woman Linda was talking about, a chic redhead with a gorgeous face and body, who had deviated from her privileged background to become one of the most sought after models in the United States. Somehow she found herself cringing at the thought of working for a man who was used to dating such lovely, glamorous women. She would constantly be wondering if he was making comparisons, which wouldn't do much to improve her own self-image.

In a voice heavy with sarcasm, she conveyed her feelings to her friend. "Thanks a lot, Lin. That piece of information has made me feel much better. Heavens, you of all people should know that just the thought of talking to a man like him terrifies me! I might as well stay home for all the good that interview's going to do me. Knowing yours truly, I'll probably become tongue-tied and make a complete fool of myself."

"If you don't try to get over that inferiority complex of yours," Linda retorted heatedly, "you're going to spend the rest of your life waiting tables at Al's Hamburger Heaven or someplace similar, Erin."

Linda was right, she thought, she was going to have to work harder at being more assertive if she wanted to get anywhere in her chosen career. Glancing across the parking lot toward the wood-and-glass structure that housed the central offices of the Piedmont Health Club, she spotted several other adjoining buildings, the entire complex surrounded by impeccably landscaped grounds.

The park-like setting should have pleased her, but when she considered the enormous price of acreage in this area what little optimism she had remaining dwindled to nothing. A sudden sensation of panic set her knees to quaking. She could tell herself that she was fully qualified to work here until the roosters stopped crowing, but that didn't make her believe it!

There she went again, she realized with a surge of self-disgust, letting negative thoughts destroy her belief in her own abilities. If she didn't pull herself together in a hurry, she was going to blow this interview before it even occurred. Straightening her back with silent determination, she tried to ignore her sick stomach and sweaty palms as she walked swiftly toward the imposing entrance of the health club.

As she arrived at her destination, she glimpsed a plant-laden lobby through the glass, with a large, modern desk situated in the center space. If the room's understated elegance hadn't been enough to increase her nervousness to unbearable proportions, the svelte brunette seated behind the desk certainly would have. She had the kind of angular figure Erin had always envied, with narrow shoulders, small breasts and a long, swan-like neck shown to advantage by the chignon she wore.

Elegantly attired in a yellow-and-beige suit which must have cost nearly as much as her roommate's Honda, the woman lifted a penciled eyebrow in bored inquiry as Erin passed through the mechanized doors and crossed the carpeted floor with the wooden precision of a marionette with its strings pulled too tight. As she drew closer, she was treated to a glacial stare which seemed to sweep her figure with supercilious disdain.

Erin swallowed past the lump of panic forming in her throat, and wondered if the brunette knew she was wearing a markdown. If her frosty gaze was any indication, Erin decided, the cost of her favorite outfit had already been calculated to the last penny. Resisting the urge to bolt, she gave the receptionist her friendliest smile with little hope of it being returned.

She wasn't disappointed. The other woman's expression remained cool and distant, her voice as frozen as her manner when she asked, "May I help you?"

Erin mumbled a greeting and told her, "I have a nine o'clock appointment with Mr. Sinclair."

Once again those contemptuous gray eyes traveled from the top of Erin's feather-cut blond hair to the tips of her bargain-basement boots, pausing to check out her ample curves along the way. This time both perfectly penciled brows rose in haughty disdain, as the woman asked, "Just what position are you applying for?"

Erin cleared her throat, certain the lump still occupying space there must be visible to the naked eye. Reminded of a pet frog she'd had as a child, she lifted her hand to cover the offending area. "I've been sent by the Liston Agency regarding the position of dietary adviser."

"Mr. Sinclair's already gone over your resumé?"

Erin's head jerked in surprise at the sharpness of the other woman's tone, and she rested her hand against her tan shoulder bag as though seeking reassurance from the supple leather. "I only applied to the agency yesterday, when they set up this interview. But I have my resumé with me."

She was confused by the prim twist of the other woman's carmined lips, unable to decide whether the alteration was a smile or a grimace. If it was a smile, she decided, it held a quality of smug satisfaction that made her distinctly uneasy. There was a rather strange cast in those cold eyes as they looked at her, one of sly calculation, which added to Erin's original impression. She decided that this woman was a nasty piece of work at the best of times, and if she wasn't mistaken this wasn't turning out to be one of the receptionist's better days.

Erin's supposition was dramatically reinforced when she was told, "I'm afraid keeping your appointment with Mr. Sinclair would be a waste of your time, Ms.—?"

"Daniels," Erin informed her tightly. "You mean the job's already been taken?"

This time the smile shifted into a pitying slant. "No, Ms. Daniels, but I'm afraid you're just not suitable."

Erin drew in a shocked breath, beginning to shake with anger as she paused to read the silver nameplate on the desk. "Since you haven't heard my qualifications, you aren't in a position to judge, Ms. Phelps."

Ms. Phelps's thin lips formed an unattractive sneer, her inexplicable dislike of Erin obvious as she snapped, "I screen all the applicants for Mr. Sinclair, and you are definitely not the person we are looking for. Now, if you don't mind I have a great deal of work to do. Good day, Ms. Daniels."

Erin slid a pointed gaze over the desktop, which was bare except for a green-felt blotter. In a voice rife with sarcasm, she muttered, "I can see you're just rushed off your feet, Ms. Phelps, but I'm afraid I'll have to insist upon your taking enough time to give me an explanation as to my unsuitability."

Long fingernails painted the same shade as that hard mouth drummed against the blotter with angry impatience, while her critical glance once again surveyed Erin's body with insulting thoroughness. "I hate to sound rude, but surely you realize an employee must provide a good example to our clientele."

This time Erin's gasp was audible, as she stared at the other woman in disbelief. That cuts it, she decided furiously. No walking clothes hanger was going to insult her and get away with it! Pushing past the startled receptionist, she headed for a nearby door marked private. As she threw open the door and propelled herself across the threshold, she was oblivious to the vitriolic abuse being meted out to her by the protesting Ms. Phelps.

Her concentration was centered on the opposite end of the room, where a man was seated behind an oak desk even larger than the one in the foyer. A plate-glass window was behind him, and the sunlight which illuminated the office temporarily blinded her. Hesitating only briefly as she blinked to clear her vision, she marched up to the man she assumed to be the club's owner.

When he indolently rose to his feet to watch her approach, she felt her throat tighten with a resurgence of panic. Although she estimated he stood just under six feet, to her he seemed like a giant. She suddenly felt like a squirrel trying to stare down a gorilla. If this was Logan Sinclair, she thought incredulously, he was without doubt the most physically intimidating male she had ever seen in her life!

It wasn't only his size, which was arresting, he was also devastatingly attractive. Thick, caramel-colored hair waved back from a broad forehead, while high, angular bones lent his tanned face distinction. His shoulders were not just broad, they were massive. A gold, short-sleeved knit shirt was stretched over his chest, and soft looking tufts of golden-brown hair emerged from the open collar. When she realized the dimensions the shirt had to cover, she marveled at the resilience of the fabric.

As her awed glance inspected his forearms, the biceps bulging with more muscle than any one man had a right to expect, she felt a prickly heat begin to flow through her midsection. Bemused by the inexplicable reaction, she returned her eyes to his face. Instantly the peculiar warmth erupted like a blast furnace, sending searing embers through every inch of her body.

The sound of a masculine throat being cleared caused her to jump like a startled rabbit. A pair of brilliant green eyes met hers with amused curiosity in their depths, and she flushed betrayingly. For a horrifying moment she became disoriented, completely forgetting why she had intruded on this man's privacy. When he shifted his weight she shivered, her attention distracted by his splendid physique. Racking her brain for something to say, she doubted if she could remember her own name with him staring at her like that.

He glanced from her to his receptionist who, although no longer screeching like a fishwife, appeared to be on the verge of apoplexy. The other woman's color was unattractively high, Erin noted with satisfaction, her thin lips twisted with barely banked rage as she glared at her. Erin found herself wondering what she had done to deserve this woman's enmity, at a loss to explain such a hateful attitude upon so short an acquaintance.

Unable to come up with any satisfactory explanation, she straightened defensively and once again turned her attention to the man standing in front of her in contemplative silence. "Are you Logan Sinclair?" she asked.

He smiled and nodded an affirmative. "I gather there's a slight problem between you and Ms. Phelps. Is it something I can help you with?"

Erin had to tilt her head back so far to look up at him, her neck began to ache. But the discomfort succeeded where willpower had failed. When the woman beside her rudely interrupted her before she had a chance to answer his question, Erin gained the impetus she needed to unlock her vocal chords. Stretching herself to her full five feet, three and three-quarter inches, she felt a reassuring surge of temper.

"My name is Erin Daniels," she retorted loudly, successfully drowning out Ms. Phelps's whining accents, "and you bet there's a problem!"

The redoubtable Ms. Phelps pushed Erin aside to appeal to her employer. "Logan, this . . . this person's behavior is irrational. She's probably high on drugs or mentally unbalanced. I was merely asking her a few questions when she went crazy. She should either find a bed in a mental ward, or enroll herself in a drug-rehabilitation program."

Erin whirled around, her fists clenched at her sides. "Let me tell you, before they take me off in a strait-jacket or dry me out I'll file a suit against you for slander.

"And you," she hissed, returning her antagonistic gaze to the man who was listening to their interchange in fascinated silence, "are prejudiced, and will be sued for unfair discrimination."

He looked startled. "Just what am I discriminating against?"

"Fat people!"

Erin propped her hands on her hips and scowled at him. Individuals with judgmental attitudes such as his and his receptionist's made her furious, and she saw no reason to hide her indignation. She might not be skinny but she possessed what were clinically considered to be perfect measurements. That she herself didn't agree with the general consensus was not the point, especially when she thought of the sacrifices she made on a daily basis to maintain her figure.

Although other women often envied her the voluptuous curves which covered her bones, the lushness of her body made her uncomfortable. She was too shy and introverted for it to be otherwise. Oh, she was well aware that having an attractive figure was desirable, but in her opinion she'd been granted too much of a good thing. She found her firmly rounded breasts, tiny waist and curved hips more of a detriment than an advantage.

Her appearance drew a great deal of attention from the opposite sex, especially when topped off with blond hair, big blue eyes and a lovely, creamy rose complexion. But unfortunately most men treated her as though her morals should match her sexy appearance. It was an attitude she deplored, since it precluded her having much in the way of intelligence.

But she hadn't always had the attention of over-amorous males, she thought with a visible wince of remembered pain. The trauma of early childhood, when she'd been quite a bit more than just pleasingly plump, returned to the forefront of her mind. She'd been teased unmercifully by the kids at school, making her life a constant torment. When she began to

starve herself, her parents had become frightened
enough to seek professional help for her, certain she
was showing signs of anorexia nervosa.

And maybe she would have made herself ill, she realized with the benefit of hindsight, if she hadn't
learned that her weight could be controlled with
proper diet and exercise. For her losing the pounds
she'd accumulated over the years had been a matter of
self-image and, in a very real context, one of emotional survival. Which was why, she thought, she had
developed an interest in becoming a dietitian fairly
early in life.

As she slimmed down, the desire to help others like
herself had grown. No one, she'd decided, should be
ostracized and humiliated because they were ignorant
of proper nutrition and the needs of their individual
body chemistry. Her eyes flashing with conviction, she
said as much to Logan Sinclair. But instead of getting
angry at her belligerent attitude, to her amazement, his
smile held open approval.

With beguiled fascination she noted the sensual appeal of that bold, masculine mouth. One corner was
tilted slightly higher than the other, and his teeth were
startlingly white against his tanned skin. "A good
many of my clients are overweight," he explained
quietly. "I help them get into shape, but that doesn't
mean I'm prejudiced against them as individuals."

He scanned her body in a swift, comprehensive ap-
praisal, before returning his attention to her face.
"Anyway, if you were referring to yourself, I doubt if
you weigh one ounce more than you should. Having
an attractive amount of flesh covering your bones is

no crime against nature, you know. In fact, quite the contrary.''

At the sound of a muffled exclamation he turned toward his receptionist, his expression hardening as he asked, ''You wish to make a comment, Lorna?''

Compressing her lips, Ms. Phelps shook her head and maintained a forbidding silence. Swiveling back to look at Erin, his voice deepened with sincerity. ''But putting personal opinion aside, I would like to reassure you on one point, at least. As long as they're reasonably neat in appearance, I hire my staff strictly on the basis of their qualifications.''

''Of course,'' he added teasingly, ''if they all looked like you I'd probably end up ridiculously over-staffed.''

Instead of reassuring her, his compliment caused Erin to tense with self-conscious awareness. It was a reaction she'd grown used to experiencing around the male population over the years, but one she was still unable to control. Her shy, retiring nature hadn't been eradicated along with her weight loss, and she'd never been able to completely overcome a need for self-effacement. A wolf whistle still made her want to hide behind the nearest bush, and suggestive comments from overamorous males made her feel like a chicken stuck in the coop with a fox.

Not that Logan Sinclair's remark had been in any way objectionable, it was her reaction to it she found shocking. Never had she been so physically affected by a man before, especially one she'd just met. She felt as though she was on fire, a tingling heat spreading from her scalp and slipping quickly into the pit of her stomach. That warmth slid lower into forbidden territory, turning her legs into two columns of mush. Stiffening her knees, she only prayed they would hold her up long enough for her to escape from this situation with her dignity intact.

Unfortunately for the state of her nervous system, Logan Sinclair wasn't paying any attention to her militant knees. His gaze had strayed to her agitatedly heaving breasts, a fact which accelerated her temper alarmingly. She ground her teeth together until her jaw ached. "I don't appreciate personal comments any more than I do being insulted by a member of your staff, Mr. Sinclair."

Ms. Phelps began a blustering protest, but was cut off in mid-spate by a swiftly raised hand and a rapier glance from her boss. The hand was lowered and he immediately resumed his inspection of Erin's mutinous features, a lambent glow bright in the depths of his jade eyes. "Would you appreciate a job with me, Ms. Daniels?"

She would appreciate almost anything with him, she decided dazedly. Wondering where that thought had come from, she gulped and hurriedly took a backward step. Too discomposed to maintain her aggressive attitude, she had to force herself to answer him with the scorn she felt his question deserved. "So much for your assurance that you hire your staff on the basis of their qualifications, Mr. Sinclair. You haven't seen mine," she concluded with derision, "or have you?"

His lips quirked revealingly. "Why, Ms. Daniels, whatever are you implying? I was merely going to suggest that we go over your resumé together."

Erin looked at him in dismay, but was unable to utter a sound. Logan Sinclair was once again staring at her mouth with what appeared to be single-minded attention to detail, which didn't do much to restore her composure. Clamping her lips tightly together, she held her breath until she thought her lungs would burst. In the tension-laden moments that followed, she didn't know whether to pass out or make a run for the door.

With touching dignity she finally straightened, unaware of the regret in her eyes. "What would be the point in continuing with this discussion, sir? As your receptionist has already informed me, I'm not right for the position."

All humor disappeared from his face in an instant, his expression grim as he turned toward Ms. Phelps. There was an underlying ring of steel in his voice as he asked softly, "She did what?"

"Logan, Ms. Daniels obviously misunderstood my intentions," the other woman exclaimed nervously. "I wasn't the one who arranged her interview, and I was merely attempting to gather the necessary information before announcing her arrival."

Erin's eyes widened at the bald-faced lie, and she uttered a disdainful snort. "I beg your pardon, but you did nothing of the sort. You told me I was wasting my time, and that I was not suitable for the position of dietary adviser because I wouldn't provide a good example to the clientele."

"As I said," Ms. Phelps insisted stiffly, "you misunderstood me."

"Whatever Lorna said or did not say to you isn't the issue here," Logan interjected quietly. "Since I'm the person doing the hiring, my opinion of you is the only one you need to worry about.''

His low tones seemed to stroke against Erin's flesh, heavy with a sensual impact that snatched at her breath. Disconcerted, she demanded, ''Then why did you tell this . . . your receptionist to screen all your applicants?''

As she voiced the question, her pointing finger came close to bopping Ms. Phelps on the nose. The other woman jumped back with an affronted squeal. Logan's eyes followed the movement. ''Would you care to answer that question, Lorna?''

''Logan, I only . . .'' Her voice was disgustingly ingratiating, holding a simpering pleading note that grated on Erin's nerves.

''You only overstepped your duties,'' he interrupted, the ominous calm of his voice boding ill for the distressed woman.

''Well, yes, but I thought . . .''

He gave her a look guaranteed, in Erin's opinion, to shut up even the angel Gabriel on Judgment Day. ''We will discuss your thoughts at a later date. Right now I suggest you return to your desk. I have an interview to conduct.''

With a last glare in Erin's direction, the discomposed woman stormed out of the office in high dudgeon. Erin almost found it in her to feel sorry for her, but couldn't quite manage it. Instead she was elated by Logan Sinclair's defense of her. Standing at the door through which Ms. Phelps had disappeared, she allowed herself the tiniest smile of satisfaction.

When a masculine chuckle broke the silence, Erin turned and frowned in consternation. "What's so amusing?" she questioned uneasily.

Although he managed to control his laughter, his smile widened. "I've been watching the expressions flitting across your face. You are beginning to intrigue me, Ms. Daniels."

There was a definite hint of good-humored conjecture in his voice, and before she realized what was happening her lips began to lift in a shyly responsive grin. But suddenly his chest rose on a swiftly indrawn breath, and her smile faltered as he studied her with an intensity she didn't dare to analyze. Feeling it necessary to evade that discerning gaze, she cautiously placed a little more distance between them.

She mentally castigated herself for her behavior. She was not in the least intimidated by Logan Sinclair's stature, she told herself, either social or physical. Admittedly he made her nervous, but she was usually uptight when meeting new people. After all, hadn't she stood up for her rights against Ms. Phelps and emerged victorious? She most definitely had! But even though she assumed an assured stance and angled her head proudly, she was dismayed to feel her adrenaline-based self-confidence disappearing.

The rest oozed out of her when he asked, "Have I embarrassed you again, Ms. Daniels?"

Hastily glancing at a spot just below the open neck of his shirt, she struggled and failed to regain her composure. She was at the point of mumbling a hasty disclaimer before slinking ignominiously toward the door, when a muffled sound alerted her attention. Cautiously she peeked up at him, and stiffened with indignation when she realized he was no longer even trying to control his amusement. His shoulders were shaking with silent laughter, those beautiful dark-green eyes of his brimming with mirth at her expense.

"It seems you're taking a delight in doing so, Mr. Sinclair."

"Guilty as charged," he admitted cheerfully, "but then you shouldn't rise to the bait so readily."

His playful attitude caused her to relax a little, and she reacted accordingly. There was a slightly impish slant to her mouth as she retorted boldly, "I'm surprised someone hasn't strangled you before now."

His lips twisted in wry acknowledgement. "I'm certain my mother thought of it a time or two. I guess I was fortunate being raised for the most part by a succession of nannies."

Disturbed by the faint note of bleakness in his voice, her lashes flickered guiltily. "I'm sorry if I sounded insulting. I . . . sometimes my tongue runs away with me."

"I suffer from the same affliction, and there's no need to apologize," he responded gently. "You know, you're quite a puzzling contradiction."

Erin felt her cheeks growing hot. "I am?"

He nodded, his eyes narrowing consideringly. "You burst in here like a furiously spitting cat, but now you don't quite seem to know what to do with yourself."

Growing warmer by the minute, she whispered, "I'm not at my best during interviews."

"Now that surprises me," he said. "From the way you routed my receptionist, I would have thought you intrepid enough to handle any situation."

She glanced at him from eyes sparkling with mirth, and allowed her mouth to form the tiniest curve. "I don't usually lose my temper, but Ms. Phelps rubbed me the wrong way."

"Then remind me never to make the same mistake," he drawled with an exaggerated shudder.

The thought of him rubbing her in any way at all caused her to avert her head hastily, and there was a revealing pause before he spoke. "Hey, you're really very shy, aren't you?"

"Painfully so at times," she responded in a disgusted tone. "It's a handicap I keep trying to overcome, but without much success. The best I've managed to do so far is cover it up."

Although she realized her answer could very well cause him to question the advisability of hiring her, something in Logan Sinclair's manner compelled her to be completely truthful and up front with him. His reaction to Ms. Phelps's attempt to escape being called on the carpet for her behavior had shown Erin a man who wouldn't appreciate dishonesty or subterfuge in any form, and it was an attitude she respected.

Apparently her deductions were correct, because he seemed pleased by her openness. "And are you successful at hiding the evidence of such a disgraceful character flaw?"

With a glance that spoke volumes, she retorted, "Usually—unless I'm being teased."

"I see," he said solemnly, without blinking an eye. He studied her for a moment before crossing his arms over his chest. "Then I'm afraid we've got a definite problem on our hands, Ms. Daniels."

Two

Trying not to show her disappointment, Erin lowered her gaze and gave a resigned nod of acceptance. "I can understand if you're worried about my ability to handle working with the public."

"That's not it, at all. If you want the truth, it's me I'm worried about."

Startled, she asked, "You? But I ... I don't understand."

"Then let me explain," he said, his expression serious. "You see, I suffer from a certain ... personality quirk. I don't know whether I was born this way or if I was dropped on my head as a baby, but I'm afraid I'm a terrible tease."

With a gasp that was caught somewhere between laughter and disapproval, Erin eyed him with certainty. "It's my guess you were dropped on your head, Mr. Sinclair."

"Logan," he told her softly.

She repeated his name with a conciliatory smile. "Logan."

"And I have your permission to call you Erin?"

Her voice nearly inaudible, she whispered, "You do."

"Good!"

Logan gestured to an armchair placed in front of his desk, and Erin automatically acceded to his unspoken request. Once she was seated, he balanced his weight on the desk's edge. She quickly glanced away from his splayed thighs, feeling her heart give a curious little kick against the wall of her chest. His trim-fitting slacks clung lovingly to his bulging musculature, emphasizing the length of his legs. Nervously choosing to concentrate on a seascape mounted on the wall over his right shoulder, she bathed her drying lips with the tip of her tongue.

Logan's eyes followed the movement, and it took him a few minutes to remember what he wanted to say. When he did, his exclamation was uttered more heartily than was absolutely necessary. "Well, Erin, now that we've gotten past the true confessions, what do you say we get on with this interview?"

Before she could press her lips together, a giggle emerged, and when she looked guilty Logan's own laughter erupted. A shared appreciation of the ridiculous seemed to draw them together, and she felt a sensation closely resembling panic. A woman would have to be dead from the neck down to fight this man's charisma, she decided weakly. He was gorgeous, his sense of humor was delightful, and she didn't even mind his teasing. Well, she amended with an inward smile, not much!

Finally managing to catch her breath, she said, "We have deviated from your original intention slightly, haven't we?"

Logan's eyebrows rose at such a gross understatement. She was trying very hard to impress him, he thought, and she was obviously unaware of how absolutely adorable her earnest expression made her appear. It was all he could do to suppress another laugh, but he was afraid he would hurt her pride if he gave in to the impulse. He was pleased by Ms. Erin Daniels's forthright attitude, and he wouldn't want her to imagine otherwise.

Although he suitably schooled his features, it didn't prevent him from thinking how long it had been since he'd been with a woman and laughed with any real spontaneity. His relationships to date had been brief and basically empty of any real emotion. Outside of bed, it had been a very long time since he'd enjoyed himself with a woman, at all.

But from the moment she entered his office, he'd known that this woman was different from the rest. There was an innocence in those bright blue eyes of hers, one which went beyond the physical. It was a sensitivity of spirit that enchanted him, and magically dispersed the defenses he'd raised to guard his emotions over the years. His mother had taught him how far some women would go to satisfy their greed for power and possessions, and as a result he didn't trust easily. Yet Erin seemed to have pierced that cold, empty place inside of him. He didn't know whether to be alarmed or pleased, and decided that maybe a little of both was in order.

His attention strayed to her velvety lips, and he grabbed onto the edge of his desk with both hands. God! That mouth of hers was enough to drive a man beyond the brink of sanity. His knuckles whitened from the force of his grip, and he cleared his throat of the sudden obstruction that had centered there. "Do you have a resumé with you?"

Erin nodded, and her head continued to bounce up and down like one of those bobble toys people placed in the back windows of their cars. She blinked rapidly, dismayed by her lack of poise. With as casual a gesture as she could manage, she reached into her purse and found the necessary papers. "Certainly, Mr. Sinclair."

"Logan," he reminded her.

"Logan," she intoned with stilted politeness, handing over her resumé. "I hope my qualifications meet your approval."

While he withdrew the information from the envelope, Erin ducked her head and began twisting the strap on her purse. Realizing she was only drawing attention to her trembling hands, she pressed them against her lap. She wanted to search his features while he read, but didn't have the courage. She would know his opinion soon enough, she thought, while an all-too-familiar feeling of inadequacy caused her to squirm uneasily in the chair.

"Erin, you're an answer to a prayer."

Her eyes leaped to meet his. "You are . . . I mean, I am?"

"Most definitely. Your grades are excellent, and I'm especially pleased to note the advanced psychology classes you've taken. They will help you gain a better than average understanding of our customers' needs."

"Then..." She paused, her expression hopeful. "Then I've got the job?"

"It's yours if you want it."

She slipped to the edge of her chair and held out her hand, her eyes glowing with excitement. "You won't be sorry for giving me this chance to prove myself, Mr. Sin... I mean Logan."

With a deep-throated rumble of laughter he dropped the papers he held on top of his desk, and caught her hand between both of his. Erin's heart nearly came to a complete stop, before it rapidly regained enough rhythm to beat her to death. Noting the sudden panic which leaped to life in her eyes, he drawled, "Surely you're not still nervous of me?"

Determined not to be taken in again by his particular brand of teasing, she scoffed, "Of course not!"

She shivered when his fingertips began to smooth her palm, but the movements were accompanied by such a thoughtful, absentminded look, she gazed at him quizzically from beneath her lashes. "Umm, ahh... when do you want me to start work?"

Pleased by her stammering eagerness, he crossed his legs and linked his fingers together around his raised knee. "Haven't you forgotten something?"

Her brows peaked in puzzlement. "I don't think so."

"Aren't you going to ask me how much I'll be paying you?"

"Oh, of course." As obediently as a well-mannered child, she asked, "What will my salary be, Logan?"

He mentioned a figure that caused her to stare at him in disbelief. "What . . . ?" She cleared the squeak from her voice and tried again. "How much did you say?"

Logan repeated the amount, and Erin's lips parted on a soundless gasp. Realizing her mouth was open, she snapped it closed. Her throat felt as though she was breathing through cotton balls, her eyes wide and questioning as they searched his own. As inconspicuously as possible, she released the top button of her tailored white blouse. "This is p-probably presumptuous of me, c-considering I know next to nothing about your b-business dealings," she stammered nervously, "but isn't that a rather exorbitant amount to pay a dietitian?"

"In the general sense, but then you won't just be working here, Erin."

Astonishment colored her voice. "I won't?"

"I have more than one health club in operation throughout the state, as well as a few standardly run gyms. I would like them all to benefit from your expertise."

"How many are there in all?" she questioned matter-of-factly.

"Fifteen."

Her voice faltered. "Did you say fifteen?"

"Yes. So you see, this will be a large-scale operation. Your main duty will be to formulate the most comprehensive method of dietary analysis for our clients as a whole, which we will then combine with a similar procedure for defining appropriate exercise programs for each individual.''

Erin's stillness reflected a sudden surge of panic. Doubt crept into her mind to whittle away at her self-confidence, as the full realization of what this man expected from her hit her with the force of a blow to the solar plexis. She was both scared and excited, but for the moment fear held the upper hand. She had been well trained, yet she had no practical experience to draw on. Could she do it? she asked herself. Was she capable of undertaking the responsibility for such an enormous project?

But Logan seemed to have no doubts as to her ability, she realized, reassured by his matter of fact attitude as he continued. "Some of our clients will be overweight, some underweight, and some fairly fit who simply want to improve their stamina or their figures. These variables will require us to implement several beginning levels, with allowances being made for any serious health problems we might encounter along the way. To be precise, we'll be developing a kind of screening process for the general public."

Erin nodded absently, a contemplative frown scoring her smooth forehead. "I don't know much about exercise, except in relation to myself."

"That will be my department," he replied, "and there's the catch to all of this, Erin. We'll need to train key staff members to carry out the new program, and I'm afraid you'll be expected to travel a great deal with me. Will that pose any problems for you?"

"Oh, no," she responded breathlessly as pleasure feathered her spine. "I've always wanted to see new places."

"What about your parents?" he questioned doubtfully. "I don't know if I'd approve of my daughter traveling around the state with her boss."

Her eyes widened in surprise. "I'm twenty-three years old, not three. What I do with my life is my business, but I can assure you that I've been raised to take care of myself. My dad isn't a worldly man, but he values independence. He's never been able to leave our farm in Idaho for long, but he's a great armchair traveler. He'll be pleased that I'm being given the opportunity to expand my horizons."

He gave her a considering look. "So you're an Idaho farm girl. That must account for your peaches-and-cream complexion."

"It also accounts for my appalling shyness and lack of sophistication," she admitted ruefully. "We lived quite a distance from town, and being an only child I was used to a quiet, orderly existence. Kindergarten was something of a cultural upheaval for me, and I'm afraid I never quite recovered from the shock."

"You didn't enjoy school?"

"I loved my studies, but when it came to social graces I was a walking disaster."

"That's strange," he murmured, his eyes twinkling beneath arched brows. "I can imagine you as senior-class president, or head of the debating team, or at the very least a perky cheerleader."

Erin's laughter pealed forth unrestrainedly, her golden hair whipping against her cheeks as she shook her head. "You're way out in left field with that one, Logan. You see before you an individual commonly referred to as a geek. Oh, Lord," she gasped with another splutter of mirth, "I don't know why in the world I'm telling you all this."

"Will you feel better if I admit that I, too, also . . . ahh . . . marched to the tune of a different drummer in my youth?"

Her curiosity piqued, she studied him in silence for a moment. "I can't picture you being shy or awkward, and I bet you didn't spend most of your free time in the school library with your nose buried in a book."

He made a noise in his throat which came perilously close to choking him, a dark tide of color sweeping beneath his cheekbones as he coughed into his hand. Pausing to regain his breath, his mouth twisted with cynical amusement. "No, I spent most of my free time raising hell."

He paused briefly, a wicked gleam dancing in his eyes. "Aren't you going to ask for specifics?"

"I wouldn't dare!"

"You disappoint me, Erin."

She straightened and frowned at him indignantly. "I don't see why."

"The way you stood up to Lorna I thought you had the courage of a lion."

Made distinctly uncomfortable at the reminder, Erin muttered, "Well, now you know I really have the backbone of a mouse."

"But you're still coming to work for me, little mouse?"

With a wide grin she jumped to her feet and nodded. "Yes, thank you. I'll do my best to satisfy your requirements, Logan."

Logan wanted to assure her that satisfying him wouldn't be at all difficult, but when he realized just how that would sound he bit back the words in time. Hiding his embarrassment at the near slip, he walked with her to the door. "Be here at eight o'clock Monday morning, and I'll give you the grand tour, Erin."

"You don't want me to start tomorrow?"

He shook his head. "Give yourself this weekend to rest up. Believe me, it may be the last one you'll be able to enjoy for quite a while."

"But I don't mind," she argued. "If you need me..."

With a gentle smile and another negative shake of his head, Logan watched as Erin walked across the lobby. With every step she took away from him, the last words she'd spoken reverberated in his mind. He already needed her, he thought, thoroughly shaken by the realization. He needed her warmth and her laughter to bring brightness to his life, and he needed the touch of her hands on his body to ease the ache he felt when he was close to her. As he closed his office door, he wondered if he needed too much from Ms. Erin Daniels.

On Monday morning Erin was awake long before her alarm went off, her body tense with anticipation as she contemplated her first day as a member of Logan's staff. She squinted at the illuminated dial of the small clock on her nightstand in disbelief, wondering why time seemed to crawl when a person was looking forward to something. Normally if she awakened before sunrise, she would have buried her head under the pillow and drifted back to sleep. But today her mind was too active to allow her such a luxury.

She was understandably nervous, and considered the day ahead of her with both anticipation and dread. Anticipation because she would finally be working at the career she'd trained so hard for, and dread in case she proved to be inadequate for the job. With a grunt of self-disgust at the negative direction her thoughts were taking, she pushed back the covers and bounded out of bed.

Lying around imagining all the ways she might prove to be unsuitable for the position she was to fill was senseless. What was needed was a positive action, and she eagerly began the series of exercises she adhered to religiously each morning. The normal routine began to relieve some of her tension, and with every bend and twist she muttered a familiar litany. "I am confident, I am capable, I am self-assured."

Eventually refreshed in body if not completely in mind, she pressed the alarm button to its off position before it had a chance to wake up Linda. The wall between their rooms was paper-thin, and her friend had returned late last night from a visit to her parents. She wasn't due at the clinic until noon today, and this would give her the perfect opportunity to indulge in her favorite occupation. Erin had never known anyone who enjoyed sleeping as much as Linda.

Leaving her bedroom, she shivered as she walked down the short hallway toward the bathroom. The June weather was as capricious as early spring, blowing hot one moment and cold the next. This apartment was one of four conversions, located in what used to be a stately Berkeley home. As was often the case, the old place lacked central heating and was quite drafty on occasion.

As if to prove a point, her teeth were chattering by the time she slipped off her pajamas and pulled aside the shower curtain. After adjusting the water to a satisfactory temperature, she stepped into the ancient claw-footed tub and began vigorously soaping herself. She sighed with pleasure as the hot water pummeled her tense shoulder muscles. Leaning back, she let the soothing spray pour over her head.

She closed her eyes and breathed deeply as she began to lather her hair, enjoying the delicate aroma of the jasmine-scented shampoo which permeated the air. But suddenly Logan Sinclair's bold, masculine features implanted themselves behind her eyelids, and any lingering lassitude completely deserted her. It was almost as though he'd entered the shower with her, and a delicious tingling sensation spread through her body at the thought.

Tilting her head back to rinse the foamy suds from her hair, she gave an inelegant sniff at her foolishness. Water immediately rushed up her nose, causing her eyes to tear and her throat to close. Once her coughing jag had subsided, she groaned in disgust. "Serves you right, you idiot!"

Still grousing at her own stupidity, she shut off the faucet and grabbed a towel from the nearby rack. After sketchily drying herself she stepped from the tub, and dumped her pajamas and lingerie in the wicker hamper adjacent to the toilet. As she leaned over the washbasin, she began wiping the steam from the mirror overhead. Impulsively she stuck her tongue out at her scowling image. Uttering an embarrassed laugh,

she completed her morning ablutions in a lighter frame
of mind.

With her teeth brushed, the little makeup she used
in place and her damp hair combed into order to dry
naturally, she redonned her robe and returned to her
room. Dressing took very little time, since she'd already chosen to wear a simple yet elegantly con-
structed two-piece suit made of wrinkle-resistant
cotton. She was confident that the tailored lines flattered her full figure, and it would be cool in the pre-
dicted heat of the afternoon. So far there'd been no
mention of her wearing a leotard at work, and she
certainly wasn't going to be the one to mention the
oversight.

"Good morning," a pleasant voice rang out as she
crossed the living-room floor, her heels tapping a
warning of her approach on the hardwood surface.

Erin paused under the arched entry to the kitchen,
surprised to find her roommate busy at the stove.
"Good morning, Lin. What are you doing up this
early?"

The other woman turned and waved a spatula in the
air. "You didn't think I was going to let you leave for
your first day on the job without my assistance, did
you? Grab a cup of coffee and have a seat. There are
blueberry muffins in the bun warmer, and the eggs will
be done in a minute."

Touched by her friend's thoughtfulness, Erin
paused to give her a grateful hug before filling her favorite mug and seating herself behind their round,
glass-topped kitchen table. She glanced around the
bright yellow room, and felt distinctly comforted.
"You don't know how glad I am to have someone to

talk to this morning," she admitted. "I'm so uptight I'm about ready to jump out of my skin."

Placing a platter of scrambled eggs on the table, Linda grinned and reminded her of a similar occasion. "You did the same for me on my first day."

"Yes, but you were as cool as the proverbial cucumber."

Scooping some eggs onto her plate, the other woman grimaced wryly and shook her head. "You only thought I was calm and collected. I never told you this, but after you left for the old Hamburger Heaven that morning I promptly threw up my breakfast. By the time I got to the clinic that day I felt as if I'd died and they had forgotten to bury me."

Bypassing the eggs with a visible shudder, Erin took a reviving sip of coffee and chuckled softly. "So this was just your chance to get even?"

Linda lifted a buttered muffin in a jaunty salute. "At least I didn't fix you pancakes dripping in maple syrup!"

Erin grinned. "Can I help it if your favorite breakfast is a nutritional disaster?"

"Spoken like a born dietitian," Linda retorted. "You're going to make Logan Sinclair a very happy man, my friend."

When Erin entered the health club and crossed the lobby, she only hoped Linda's confidence in her abilities would be justified. But right at this moment she was too concerned with keeping down the coffee and muffin she'd eaten to worry overmuch about the future. She was looking forward to viewing the rest of the complex with Logan, although the prospect of

seeing him again didn't do much to calm the butterflies wreaking havoc with her stomach.

Walking up to the reception desk, she was relieved
to find a stranger sitting there. She had dreaded con-
fronting the antagonistic Ms. Phelps, and briefly
wondered if the other woman had been fired. She was
shocked at how pleasing she found the prospect, and
silently castigated herself for such unaccustomed ran-
cor. Ms. Phelps might be a bitchy pain in the behind,
but that didn't mean Erin had to start emulating her.

Some of her guilt was eased when she noticed the
silver nameplate still in place on the desktop, assuring
her that Ms. Phelps's replacement was a temporary
one. When Erin mentioned her name, the bright-eyed
young woman seated in the cushioned swivel chair
smiled vivaciously, her short brown curls bobbing as
she nodded an acknowledgement. "Logan said to send
you in the moment you arrived, Ms. Daniels."

"Thank you."

Leading her to the door of Logan's office, the temporary receptionist gave her a sidelong glance. "My
name is Carrie Marshall, and I'd like to welcome you
to the staff. We're a great bunch when you get to know
us, and I hope you'll be happy here. If I can be of any
assistance, just let me know."

"Please . . . call me Erin."

"You got it," Carrie quipped with unaffected
friendliness.

Without pausing to consider her words, Erin
blurted, "I must say, you're a big improvement over
Ms. Phelps."

Carrie uttered a pealing laugh when Erin clapped
her hand over her mouth, appalled by the uninten-

tionally rude comment. But much to her relief, Carrie merely wrinkled her pert nose and shrugged. "Don't be embarrassed by a little plain speaking, Erin. Around here, we call call her Ms. Phelps to her face and the Dragon Lady behind her back. If that woman had her way, Logan wouldn't make a move without her tripping along on his heels. She guards him with the tenacity of a bulldog."

The word picture was more than Erin could stand, and laughter bubbled up in her throat. Soon her giggles were joined by Carrie's, their mirth echoing off the walls of the cavernous reception area. When the door to the office was thrust open, Erin faltered in mid-giggle and stared dumbly at the amused expression on the face of the man who stood there. The chiseled perfection of his firm mouth had softened, the bottom lip fully and sensually provocative. As though tracing its outline in her mind, she moistened her own lips with the tip of her tongue.

Logan drew in a shocked breath, unprepared for the way his body reacted to the sight of that small, pink tongue. He had almost convinced himself that he had imagined his initial reaction to this woman, but the attraction was stronger than ever. He hadn't counted on the tremendous impact of wide blue eyes and a delicate face framed by a golden halo of hair, or of a smile sweet enough to make the angels sing.

He cleared his throat. "From the way you're enjoying yourselves, I take it I don't have to introduce you two."

The sound of his deep, husky voice caused a strange lassitude to envelope Erin's mind, and her body automatically tensed to negate the effect. Her throat nearly closed completely when she tried to swallow. Her hands were hidden behind her back, the fingers clenched so tightly her nails were digging into the soft flesh of her palms.

She clumsily caught the shoulder strap of her purse before it could fall off her shoulder. "Carrie has made me feel right at home."

Logan winked at the other woman. "She's one of the best, which is why she's being trained to replace my secretary." Unable to resist temptation, he added, "Caroline couldn't fit behind her desk any longer."

As he knew she would, Erin immediately bristled. "She had a weight problem?"

He nodded soberly, and immediately spoiled the effect by grinning at her. "The nine-month kind."

Carrie's brown eyes twinkled as she took note of Erin's chagrined expression. "Don't mind him," she advised. "You'll get used to him eventually."

An envious sigh issued from Erin's mouth as she noticed the woman's relaxed manner with Logan. Far from being intimidated, the irrepressible Carrie just shook her head at him in mocking reproof and waved a hand in Erin's direction. "I think you've picked a winner, boss. If it makes any difference, I like her a lot."

"So I see," he murmured softly, "and I'm happy you approve. Thanks, Carrie."

Logan swiveled his head, his expression understanding as he noticed the apprehension his newest employee was trying to hide. "Well, are you ready to be thrown in at the deep end?"

She inclined her head jerkily, her own smile more of a sickly grimace. With what dignity she could dredge up from the depths of her nonexistent sangfroid, she said, "I guess I'm as ready as I'll ever be."

"There's no need to look so terrified, little mouse." His brows formed a devilish arch. "I don't bite, unless I'm asked nicely."

Erin chose to ignore the double entendre, although she could feel her cheeks begin to prickle with heat at the mere idea of those white teeth nibbling at her flesh. Desperate to conceal her thoughts, she decided that in this instance attack was the best means of defense. Pursing her lips primly, she glanced at Carrie. "Is he always like this?"

Carrie placed one hand over her heart and stuck the other in the air. "I plead the Fifth."

The look in Logan's eyes was a mite too innocent to be believable, and Erin smirked up at him with a confidence she was far from feeling. "I may be a little on the cowardly side, but be warned. I can bite back if the occasion arises."

"I'm looking forward to it," he whispered huskily, an unholy glint in his eyes.

Erin heard a gasp and a muffled giggle from the woman at her side, and a new wave of heat rose from her neck to flood her face with vivid color. She almost sagged with relief when Carrie announced, "Whoops, that's my phone ringing. How about having lunch with me today, Erin?"

Erin was too disconcerted to do more than nod, but luckily Carrie was running across the floor and didn't seem to expect more of an acknowledgement from her. With a wave, she called out, "Meet you here at twelve-thirty. Bye, Logan."

Logan shook his head ruefully, a slight compression to his lips. "I was planning to take you to lunch myself."

"I...I didn't realise you would want to work through lunch."

"Who said anything about working?"

Once more Erin had trouble swallowing, the pebble in her throat having grown into a boulder. He was doing it again, she realized uncomfortably, not quite certain how to react to him. Was he carelessly living up to his playboy image, or was that sincere interest she saw in his eyes when he looked at her? Whether it was or not, she was stunned by how vulnerable she felt with him. If what Linda had told her of his reputation with women had any basis in fact, she was going to have to be careful not to let him affect her emotions to this extent.

Steadying her breathing through sheer effort of will, she whispered, "Are you ready to start the grand tour now?"

With a smile captivating enough to make her forget her recent resolution, he took her by the arm and began guiding her across the lobby. "It will be my pleasure."

There was a relaxed atmosphere throughout the complex, aided by bright, colorful murals on the walls and simple but comfortable furnishings. But it was the exercise facilities which most delighted her. The gym and pool area acted as a hub, around which were located showers and dressing rooms. The corridor walls were lined with row after row of convenient combination lockers, and there was an impressive array of equipment spotted throughout the huge room.

Erin gestured toward the dividing wall between the gym and pool area, which was comprised entirely of glass. "Whoever designed this building must have had a sadistic streak a mile wide."

Logan appeared startled. "What makes you say that?"

"Don't you think it's cruel to force your customers to view all that cool, luscious water while they're sweating and panting in an attempt to shape up?"

"I admit I never thought of it when I drew up the plans."

She gave a moan of dismay. "Ohh, why do I always end up with my foot in my mouth?"

Her contrite expression was too much for Logan. He began to whoop with laughter, his hilarity increasing when she pursed her lips into an affronted pout. The people around them stared at her reddening face with a combination of amusement and sympathy, which only increased her embarrassment. Although she could see the amusing side of this confrontation, when she glanced at Logan she experienced the strongest urge to kick him in the shins.

The last building they inspected housed a massage-and-tanning parlor, which shared space with a small boutique where sweats, leisure clothes, bathing suits, leotards and wraps were sold. There was even a self-serve deli, of sorts, where machines offered nutritious salads, juices and high-energy snacks. Buying each of them a canned drink, Logan motioned her to follow him outside to one of several umbrella-covered patio tables placed on a semicircle of lawn.

Erin sat down next to him, sighing as she surveyed her surroundings. "This place is a health fanatic's paradise."

To her amazement Logan became quite flustered by the compliment, and looked so boyishly proud of himself that she instantly forgave him for his earlier amusement at her expense. She laughed, and he grinned sheepishly. "It's the culmination of a dream I shared with a friend a long time ago."

Logan crossed his arms on top of the table, and gazed at her consideringly. "You know, there's something about you that reminds me of him. Maybe it's your feisty stubbornness."

Her mouth curved with irrepressible humor. "I am not stubborn!"

"Is that why it took me so long to convince you to come to work for me?"

"It didn't take all that long," she argued. "Anyway, I suspect you have very little trouble finding ways to get what you want."

Logan leaned across the table and ran a caressing finger down her cheek. "Not always," he said quietly, "but then some things are worth a little extra effort, Erin."

Her chest rose on a shaken breath as she stared in fascination at the darker flecks in his green eyes. "What things?"

"I'll tell you tonight during dinner."

"I don't remember agreeing to have dinner with you."

"But you will," he murmured with certainty. "I'll pick you up at seven-thirty, all right?"

"Don't get involved," an inner voice warned. "This man is way out of your league and you know it!" But for once Erin wasn't prepared to be sensible, her longing to be with Logan obliterating the voice of caution from her mind. "Seven-thirty will be fine," she whispered shyly.

Three

___

Logan wasn't certain what to expect when he arrived at Erin's apartment. He had sensed her momentary hesitancy when she'd accepted his dinner invitation, and the memory made him uneasy. What in the hell was he doing, he asked himself in disgust? Couldn't he at least have given her a chance to know him a little better before putting the rush on her? He was acting like a callow youth without the sense God gave a mosquito, and at the comparison his mouth tilted in amusement. She had stung him where it hurt and made him itch and burn all right, but if he had his way she was soon going to share his discomfort.

As he climbed the stairs to her apartment, just the thought of having his way with Erin was enough to cause his respiratory system to go haywire. He resisted the urge to loosen his tie, and as he reached the second-floor landing he wondered if he was in as good a physical condition as he imagined. Mentally he was a total loss, that was for sure. Since a certain young woman had entered his life, he hadn't been able to do much more than moon around with a sappy grin on his face.

The blue silk dress shirt he was wearing beneath his cream suit jacket was designed for summer coolness, yet he felt uncomfortably stifled. If his suspicions were correct, it was probably a guilty conscience making him sweat. He laughed with self-mocking derision, and there was still a sardonic curve to his mouth as he pressed Erin's front-door bell to announce his arrival. He should feel guilty, he decided, since the images which formed in his mind when he thought of how he wanted this evening to end were far from innocent. What was happening to him? He and Erin were little more than strangers, and yet he already wanted her with an intensity he found faintly shocking.

That tempting bit of womanhood had burrowed right under his skin, and it really shook him up to realize that he wanted more from her than just a sexual relationship. That was all he had ever wanted or needed from the other women he'd known through the years, and these new feelings confused him. They also made him damn nervous! Hadn't he seen what loving a woman had done to his father, who had eventually been stripped of both his manhood and his pride? No, he wanted no part of that so-called tender emotion, thank you very much! He wasn't going to allow himself to become vulnerable to that extent.

Who was he kidding? The question formed in his mind, and was analyzed with an honesty based on the cynicism toward the female of the species he'd developed over the years. Erin threatened his self-control in a way he found difficult to understand, let alone to accept. From the moment she'd burst into his office he'd been aware of everything about her, almost as though something in her had called out to him. Although the strength of his attraction to her wasn't a reality he welcomed, he knew it was one he couldn't deny. Right now he was as uptight as a boy anticipating being with his first woman, and when he considered his age and experience it made him feel like a fool.

But all Logan's doubts fled the moment the door opened and a mellow glow from a shaded living-room lamp bathed Erin in its gentle radiance. His eyes drank in the sight of her with rapacious hunger, and the rhythm of his pulse picked up until he could hardly breathe. She was wearing a gold halter-necked dress in a silky fabric that caressed her body the way his hands ached to do. The light, shimmery material seemed to blend with the baby fine hair which brushed her bare shoulders, giving her the appearance of a golden goddess.

"You look beautiful," he murmured.

"Thank you." Her gaze studied the contrast made by his light-colored suit and tie and the blue silk shirt he wore. She smiled tightly, and returned his approval in a nervous rush. "You look very nice, too."

Although stilted, the compliment pleased him a great deal more than more effusive ones he'd received from women in the past. He wanted Erin to find him attractive; to be as drawn to him as he was to her.

There was a need growing within him, and he wanted to please her in ways that would make her forget any other man who had ever touched her. It was desire in its purest form, emotional as well as physical, and it made him feel exposed and vulnerable to the sweet-faced woman watching him so intently. "Are you ready to go?"

The sudden curtness in his voice caused Erin to recoil slightly, and in an attempt to conceal her unease she gestured toward a nearby hall stand. "Just let me get my purse."

She smoothed her hands down her sides as she crossed the entry, hoping Logan wouldn't notice how badly her fingers were shaking. With self-conscious abruptness she grabbed the dangly chain of her gold sequined evening bag, slipping it over her wrist as she strived for a nonchalance she feared was beyond her ability to project. "Would y-you like to come in for a drink?"

As she glanced over her shoulder at Logan, the apprehension in her gaze made him feel like a heel for snapping at her. There was no way she could know that he was impatient with himself and not with her. It wasn't her fault she threw him so far off kilter, he thought with self-imposed irritation.

Quite the contrary, since she'd never reacted to him with more than shy friendliness. That realization wasn't doing his ego much good, but was this compulsion he felt to make her aware of him as a desirable man merely ego? Or did it stem, as he suspected, from a deeper need he'd never been aware of until now?

Logan didn't want to consider the ramifications of that question, and quickly shook his head. "It's late and you must be starving, so why don't I take a rain check on that drink?"

Erin was too relieved by his refusal to do more than nod. Just the thought of being alone with him in her apartment was enough to increase her nervousness to alarming proportions. Yet even while cursing her own naïveté, she was honest enough to accept her lack of sophistication as an integral part of her personality. As she turned away from Logan to lock the door of her apartment, she was shocked by how badly she wished it could be otherwise. If she were more worldly, more like the women he was used to dating, she thought longingly, he might become attracted to more than her credentials as a dietitian.

They had negotiated the stairs and were exiting the front door when Logan asked if she liked Mexican food. "Yes, I think it's great," she admitted with real enthusiasm. "My dad's originally from Texas, where he became a Mexican food junkie. When he introduced me to the spicy dishes and red-hot salsa—it was love at first bite."

A sporty metallic-blue Thunderbird was parked at the curb, and as he opened the passenger door for her his gaze dropped to her slightly parted lips. Erin quickly ducked her head and seated herself, her heart vibrating in staccato beats that threatened to bruise the wall of her chest. As he circled the car to reach the driver's side, Erin used the short time available to try to get a grip on her runaway emotions. It wasn't easy, when even the sight of his graceful, loose-hipped stride was enough to make her shiver with awareness.

Logan drove into the center of Berkeley, his long-fingered hands firmly wrapped around the steering wheel as he talked casually with Erin. After a few minutes she seemed less tense, and he silently congratulated himself on his acting ability. It was a good thing she couldn't read his mind, he decided with amusement. One hint of his thoughts and she'd probably leap out of the car and throw herself in front of oncoming traffic.

Her closeness was causing his body to send out unmistakable signals. His heartbeat was rapid, his breathing constricted, and his muscles rigid as he subdued the need to reach out and touch her. The light, floral scent she wore was teasing his nostrils with its delicate aroma, and it was all he could do to keep his eyes on the road and his hands to himself. Oh, but she was a lovely distraction!

When Logan slowed his speed and unexpectedly pulled into a graveled drive, Erin looked about her in surprise. The narrow alleyway they were passing through was located in one of the older and less salubrious sections of the city, and she gazed doubtfully at the colorful graffiti which embellished the seedy-looking building they parked beside. Every conceivable inch of space on the wall had been whitewashed and painted with vivid, oversized murals depicting bullfighting scenes. The effect was colorful, if a bit graphic.

Logan turned toward her and laughed at the dazed expression on her face. "Not what you expected?"

Still staring at the wall in fascination, she admitted, "Not exactly, but it's certainly different."

"Trust me," he advised as he threw open his door. "It may not be much to look at, but you won't find better Mexican food anywhere else in town."

"How did you find this place?" she asked as he helped her from the car. "There wasn't even a sign visible from the street."

"They don't need one. The Lopez family opened this restaurant nearly thirty years ago, and the only advertisement they've ever had to depend on is word-of-mouth. Their customers are loyal to the point of fanaticism."

Erin peeked up at him through her long, gold-tipped lashes and laughed. "And you're included in their number?"

"I'm one of the ringleaders," he replied with a grin. "I've been coming here since my college days. Manny Lopez and I were UCB fraternity brothers, and I spent a lot of time being stuffed to the eyeballs by his mother. Mama Beatrice had the idea that all young boys were starving to death."

"And were you?"

"Only for affection," he responded quietly. "I envied Manny his mother. Mama Beatrice gave out hugs as amply as she did food."

They had reached the entrance, and Logan paused with his hand on the ornately crafted wrought-iron handle which was bolted into a thick, heavily carved door. He looked down at her, and Erin caught her breath at the brooding darkness that had entered his eyes. "Mama Beatrice typified my idea of what a mother should be. My own is basically a cold woman, and she never had the time or patience to deal with the emotional needs of a young boy.

"Of course," he continued with a hollow laugh, "I learned at an early age not to expect much from her. I don't remember how old I was the first time she told me she'd never wanted children. According to her, she only had me to provide my father with an heir. Consequently there's never been any love lost between us."

Erin gazed up at him helplessly. "I'm sorry, Logan."

"Hey, don't let it get you down," he said with more than a trace of embarrassment. "It was rough when I was a kid, but now I've learned not to expect any miracles. As adults my mother and I get along for the sake of appearances, but I don't go out of my way to visit her. In fact," he admitted as he pulled open the door, "if it weren't for my father, I doubt we'd see each other at all."

Erin's heart ached for the sad, lonely little boy he must have been. No wonder Logan was so independent and self-contained, she decided, swallowing past the lump of emotion lodged in her throat. He'd had to be to survive the emotional neglect of his childhood. She had just been given a glimpse of the real man beneath the smiling, debonair facade he presented to the world, and the loneliness she sensed inside him disturbed him in a way she hadn't expected.

She wanted to smooth away that slight frown from between his brows, and ease the tightness of his lips with her own. She wanted to reach out and hug him; to give him the kind of comfort and affection she'd generally taken for granted. Her mother and father had always lavishly supplied hugs and kisses and words of praise. Thinking of her parents, she realized how much they would like Logan. They were excellent judges of character, and had often been uncannily perceptive about her friends. Their life-styles might be totally dissimilar to his, but there was a basic goodness in the man which would bridge any gaps. The thought left a warm glow inside of her.

The interior of the restaurant was a pleasant surprise. Dozens of brilliantly hued piñatas in the shapes of birds and animals hung from the ceiling, and the adobe-colored walls held ornately framed paintings executed on black velvet. Brass-domed lights hung over each leather-backed booth, the tables covered with red-and-white checked tablecloths. The entire effect was homey and welcoming, and Erin smiled her approval.

Returning her smile, Logan placed his arm around Erin as he guided her toward the reservation desk. Without thinking, she leaned back with a small sigh of pleasure. Almost immediately she realized the penalty for relaxing her guard. In a smooth, unconsciously affectionate response, his hand slid across her back and settled at her waist. Oh, mercy! she thought as he drew her against his side. If his embrace was meant to be casual, the attempt was a dismal failure.

The firmness of his touch seemed to burn through the thin material of her dress, causing her skin to prickle with heart-thudding heat. She could feel each separate finger on his large hand, as though he was placing his brand on her. Such a fanciful thought made her wonder what it would be like to be made love to by him. She could almost feel his large, muscular body pressing her against a yielding mattress, and her cheeks caught fire at the sensations that resulted from her vivid imagination.

In an attempt to cover the visible evidence of her embarrassment, she whispered, "My, it's warm in here, isn't it?"

The smooth undulation of Erin's hip against the side of his hand as they crossed the flagstone floor was wreaking havoc with Logan's concentration, but he managed to catch her drift. Warm doesn't quite cover it babe, he mused with a stilted smile. But all he said was, "Yes, it certainly is."

Erin was hardly reassured. She was too busy cursing herself for instigating such a boringly trite note into their conversation. At this rate, she decided, nearly hyperventilating in an effort to stem the warmth invading her face, it wouldn't be long before Logan wrote her off as a puce-complexioned idiot. You have got to get a hold on yourself, Erin, she warned with unspoken, but no less demanding fervor. If you don't develop a little sophistication in a hurry, he's going to begin patting you on the head like an adoring child begging for attention.

Certain that Logan had already taken note of her obvious fascination with him, she was prepared for the worst as they stood waiting to be seated. His eyes searched her tightly drawn features, a frown creasing his forehead as he questioned her silence. "Is something bothering you, Erin?"

"No!"

Oh, God, she thought sickly, why had she squawked at him like a chicken about to have its neck wrung? He'd only asked an innocent question, for heaven's sake! She gave him a sidelong glance, but he didn't seem angry. In fact, he almost appeared to be pleased about something. Well, she certainly wasn't responsible for that smug curve to his lips, but now was not the time for clinical analysis. She was just fortunate that he'd been too preoccupied with his own thoughts to notice her asinine behavior. Briefly closing her eyes, she silently offered up a prayer of thanksgiving to an understanding God.

But before she could savor her relief, he bent down until his mouth brushed against her ear. "Don't worry, sweet thing. I don't seduce ladies in restaurants."

Her lashes flew upward, and she gasped at him with dismay at his perception. Feeling almost desperate as a tense silence lengthened between them, she said the first thing that came into her head. That it happened to be a lie didn't faze her in the least. "I never for a moment thought you did!"

"Then why are you trembling like a little green leaf in the wind?" he whispered huskily.

Doubting her ability to answer him with any degree of lucidity, she kept her mouth firmly closed. When the hostess approached with a welcoming greeting to lead them to a corner booth, Erin felt like kissing her. Her feet moved eagerly to follow the pleasant-faced woman, but she nearly moaned aloud when Logan remained glued to her side. The sinuous brush of his body against hers was threatening to give her cardiac arrest, and that slight trembling he'd referred to had deteriorated into a bad case of the shakes.

With a deep-throated chuckle, Logan gave her hip a reassuring pat that almost caused her knees to buckle. After assisting her into the booth, he gave her a mocking grin before sliding in beside her. Erin moved over for him, but glanced longingly at the empty space across the table as she did so. "Would you rather I sat over there?" he asked.

Erin bit the bullet and forced herself to relax. "Of course not," she replied with forced casualness. "This is quite cozy."

"Mmm," he murmured in agreement. "I like having you close to me."

Once again she couldn't think of a thing to say and quickly lifted the menu the hostess had placed in front of her. Logan did the same, and the next few minutes were spent discussing the various dishes available to them. By the time the waitress came to take their order, some of Erin's tension had dissipated. The low murmur of voices as the other diners conversed with each other helped her to relax, and she was finally able to turn toward the man at her side with an appreciative smile. "I like your choice of restaurant, Logan."

"I had a feeling you would," he responded quietly. "You don't strike me as the kind of woman easily impressed with external gilt and glamour."

"I'm not," she admitted wryly. "If you want the truth, that was the kind of elegant restaurant I thought you'd choose."

"Sure you're not disappointed?"

"Oh, no!" she exclaimed with a fervency that made him hide a grin behind his hand. "I would have felt about as comfortable as a beached fish."

This time Logan made no attempt to hide his amusement, and his mellow laughter completely dispelled the last of Erin's self-consciousness. Their food arrived on steaming platters, and as the meal progressed they never seemed to run out of conversation. They discussed everything from their preferences in food to their favorite hobbies and discovered that they had a great deal in common.

Like her, Logan loved to swim and spend lazy days on sandy beaches, with the roar of the waves providing nature's background music. He enjoyed watching old movies with a bowl of hot, buttered popcorn beside him, and he approved of most of today's modern music, with the exception of heavy metal. He also went horseback riding every chance he got, and even boarded a couple of his own horses at a ranch off Crow Canyon Road in Hayward.

"That's one thing I miss living in the city," she admitted. "My dad put me up on my first pony when I was five, and gave me a roan quarter horse for my thirteenth birthday. Dusty and I were nearly inseparable, and the first thing I do when I go home for a visit is saddle her up."

Logan noticed the way Erin's eyes darkened with emotion as she spoke, and wondered if they would take on that smoky violet hue when he made love to her. He drew in a swift breath, and his voice sounded slightly strained as he asked, "You named a roan Dusty?"

Although she tried to appear serious, the amused tilt at the corner of her mouth gave her away. "Provide Dusty with a bit of soft earth or a mud puddle, and she's in heaven. My dad had her all brushed and shiny-coated when he brought her home, with a big red bow tied around her neck. He backed her out of the trailer on a leading rein and that contrary animal went down with a flurry of hooves and a whinny of ecstasy. Dad was so startled he forgot to let go of the rope, and he went with her."

Erin chuckled at the memory and shook her head. "You should have seen the disgusted look on his face when she began rolling around on her back, kicking her legs in the air like an overgrown puppy. Dad was so mad he nearly turned the air blue with his cussing, but my mother was laughing too hard to yell at him for adding to my vocabulary. He was muttering something about a glue factory when he dragged Dusty off to the barn to clean her up, but for me it was love at first sight. Except for that one idiosyncracy she's sweet-natured and easy-gaited, and you couldn't ask for a more dependable saddle horse. Dad still grumbles a lot, but I've seen him sneak her a carrot or two when he thought no one was looking."

"You miss your parents a great deal, don't you, Erin?"

She sighed and nodded. "Is it so obvious?"

"To me it is," he whispered softly. "Since you're an only child, it must have been difficult for them when you went away to college."

"It was a terrible wrench for all three of us." A momentary look of remembered pain creased her mobile features. "I thought I was going to die from homesickness until Linda took me in hand. Her friendship got me through the worst of it, and talking to my parents on the phone got me through the rest. Much later my mother told me that she and Dad wanted to tell me to pack up and come home, but they knew that eventually I would adjust to being without them."

Erin's expression softened as she glanced blindly into space, her inner vision filled with the faces of her parents. "It was more important to them that I be able to fulfill my dream of becoming a dietitian, because if I didn't I would always regret what might have been. So I was encouraged to stick it out, and they constantly told me how proud of me they were for being accepted at such a prestigious university.''

Logan brushed the back of his hand down her cheek, his fingers trailing across her smooth skin until he reached her rounded chin. Cupping it gently with his palm, he turned her head in his direction. ''You were very fortunate to have had parents like that, honey. They sound extraordinarily wise and loving.''

When she met his eyes Logan released her chin, but Erin could still feel his gently consoling touch through every nerve end in her body. With a smile that held more trust than she was aware of, she leaned against him with a sigh. ''I've always known they were special, but I don't think I really appreciated them until I became an adult and could fully understand their generosity of spirit, Logan.''

''It's normal for children to take such things for granted.''

She nodded, her expression pensive. ''I was so used to coming first in their lives that I never once questioned their guidance. They believe that being a good parent means giving a child the freedom to develop their own dreams for the future, instead of trying to force them into a more acceptable mold.''

Logan held her gaze, his expression thoughtful. ''I agree with them, Erin. To me a child is like a rosebud, with all the beautiful promise of the future wrapped up in silken petals. If it's plucked from the bush too soon, or overprotected by a closed fist, it will either die or grow into a bruised, twisted parody of what it could have been.''

Erin caught her breath at the sensitivity of his comparison. ''You're going to be a wonderful father one day.''

''Sometimes I wonder about that,'' he admitted quietly. ''I'm usually good with my friends' kids, but I haven't had the best parenting example to follow. It's a good thing I plan to remain a bachelor, because I'd probably be a rotten father.''

Logan glanced down at the tablecloth, and Erin studied his bent head with painful uncertainty. Although his words had been spoken in a lightly dismissive tone, she had heard the fear and uncertainty in his voice. She ached to run soothing fingers through his hair; to draw his head to her breast in comfort. The desire to touch him was so strong, she never once thought of resisting the need for physical contact. Slowly reaching out, she rested her small hand against his broad shoulder. ''I repeat, you will make a wonderful father, Logan.''

He stiffened, and swiftly raised his head until their glances locked together. ''How can you be so certain?'' he questioned huskily.

''Because you're kind and gentle and understanding,'' she whispered, ''and you don't have to hide behind a macho image like so many men do. You will be open and aware of the needs of your children the way you are with those of your employees, because that's the sort of man you are. I know I haven't known you long, but if I'd had any doubts regarding your character they would have been wiped away at lunchtime today. The people who work for you not only respect you as an employer, Logan, they also care for you as a friend.''

Logan leaned closer and tenderly cupped her cheek in his hand. His breath was warm and soft against her mouth, his eyes as dark and deep as a forest at midnight. "And if I admit to needs of my own, Erin? Will you think less of me, if I tell you how badly I want to be alone with you right now?"

Her lashes flickered hesitantly, but a swift dart of excitement overshone the nervousness in her gaze. "I won't think any less of you, Logan."

He pressed his forehead against hers, and released his breath on a groan as his eyes closed. "Let's get out of here," he muttered hoarsely. "If I don't kiss you soon I'm going to go right out of my mind!"

Four

———

Erin knew they must have paid the bill and walked to the parking lot, but as she settled herself against the luxuriously cushioned bucket seat of Logan's blue Thunderbird, she couldn't remember doing either. She was in a confused daze, her senses on fire with a physical awareness she'd never before experienced. Not a single man she'd dated in the past had come anywhere close to having this astounding effect on her senses, and she shivered with anticipation as she watched Logan circle the car.

But suddenly the moon appeared from behind a cloud cover to illuminate their surroundings, and Erin stiffened with alarm. Logan's features seemed unusually stern, and she felt as though she was looking at a stranger. His mouth was harshly compressed and without the smile she'd come to expect. His jawline

looked rigid, and the outline of his body large and intimidating. As he drew nearer to the driver's side, she
felt herself begin to panic at the thought of being alone
with him in the close confines of the car.

She wasn't ready for this, she realized frantically.
He was too dominant, too experienced, and entirely
too much of a man to be satisfied by a novice like her.
Wouldn't he quite naturally expect more than she
could give him? He was so far out of her league, she'd
have to be an Olympic sprinter to catch up. In the restaurant when he had admitted needing to be alone with
her, she'd been so pleased and flattered by his attention that she hadn't considered the complete ramifications of the situation she was getting herself into.
What a stupid, idiotic little fool she was, she thought
in disgust. While she had been weaving romantic day-
dreams around a few anticipated kisses, he had most
likely been wondering if she'd like the color of his
sheets!

By the time Logan seated Erin in the car and strode
toward the driver's side, every muscle in his body was
rigid as he anticipated holding her in his arms. But the
instant he slammed the door behind himself and
turned toward the woman at his side, he could tell by
her expression that she was no longer of like mind.
Although the light inside the car was dim, it would
have taken a blind man to miss the frightened glitter
in her eyes.

Damn it! She hadn't just cooled off, she'd frozen
solid. Her hands were clenched tightly around her
evening bag and her mouth compressed into a tight
line when she glanced in his direction. She was looking at him as if he was Jack the Ripper, instead of a

normal man caught up in an agony of desire for her. All of the warmth and sensual promise had drained out of her face, leaving behind a pale shadow of the woman she'd been only moments ago.

Logan wondered what the hell he was going to do now. His experience had been gained with women who knew the score, not with shy, unsophisticated innocents. The answer didn't come to him in a blinding revelation, but in more of a logical if disappointed certainty. Leaving her in no doubt that he was expecting to make love to her had been a stupidly gauche move on his part. He had been too obvious in his desire for her, forgetting she wasn't the kind of woman to indulge in casual sex.

That it wouldn't be casual on his part made no difference, because it was too soon to convince her of how special she had become to him. It was too soon for a lot of things, he decided glumly. If he wanted Erin to open to him in a passionate flowering, he was going to have to nurture her budding womanhood with tenderness and care. He was also going to have to get used to frustration if he didn't want to frighten her away for good. But sweet Lord, he wanted her so much he was shaking apart inside!

He leaned forward, gripping the steering wheel until his knuckles whitened. His chest heaved as he closed his eyes and tried to calm himself, gritting his teeth against the hard urgency of his body. But his control was tentative at best, and with a muttered imprecation he rested his forehead against the backs of his hands. He wondered if mentally reciting the multiplication tables would distract his attention from the demands of the flesh, but he doubted it. He was as hot as a firecracker and just about as likely to explode.

Unfortunately Erin chose that moment to reach out to him with hesitant uncertainty, her nervousness replaced by worry. "Logan, what's wrong? Are you ill?"

At the touch of her hand on his arm, all of his good intentions flew out the window. With a low moan he reached for her, his voice tormented as he whispered, "God help me, because I can't seem to help myself. Don't let me frighten you, Erin."

"I'm not frightened."

As she whispered the reassurance, she was amazed to realize she spoke the truth. She suddenly knew he was as vulnerable to her as she was to him, and as he trembled in her arms that knowledge both delighted her and calmed her fears. She was filled with a depth of tenderness and a pervading joy so unique she wondered how she'd ever survive such happiness.

Logan drew back, his eyes tracing her features before settling on her mouth. Erin heard him draw in a shaken breath, and watched in fascination as his head slowly lowered. His sensuous mouth pressed against her own with infinite gentleness, and she sighed with delight. She could feel the contact spread sensation through her body like liquid fire, and she felt close to fainting as his arms drew her closer. The cut of her halter dress had prevented her from wearing a bra, and her breasts swelled and firmed as his circling arms pulled her fully into his embrace.

All of her doubts fled as Logan deepened the kiss, his tongue gliding smoothly over her burning lips.

"Open your mouth for me, baby," he murmured huskily. "Let me taste you."

His head was a mere breath away from her quivering mouth as he spoke, his attention covered by the stunned expression darkening her eyes. Sliding his long fingers across the satiny smoothness of her back, his touch trailed over her naked shoulders to her neck. He held her face still for his inspection, cupping her flushed cheeks with tenderness. His hands moved to thread through her hair, the strands rippling like a golden rain over his skin. "Are you all right?"

"I don't know."

A light ripple of laughter greeted her bewildered response. "Are you always this honest?"

"I don't know that, either," she admitted weakly. "I've never felt like this before."

His eyes narrowed on her slightly parted lips, a heated question in their depths as he whispered, "Do you want my mouth?"

With dazed certainty she nodded. "Then open for me," he demanded once again.

As though deaf to everything but the sound of his voice, Erin parted her lips with a hunger that shocked her. She almost cried out as his teeth and tongue nibbled and caressed her into a fever of need. His thumbs rubbed the underside of her jaw and the sensitive flesh below her small ears, while he brushed his mouth over hers in teasing forays that left her desiring more of him.

"Logan," she groaned.

He smiled against her lips. "Is this what you want?"

His low growl wafted over skin unbearably sensi-
tized by his touch, and she drew in a sobbing breath of
protest. Her hands clung to his shoulders, her fingers
digging into his jacket with impotent fervor. "Kiss me
harder, Logan."

This time she felt his mouth all the way to her toes,
and her cry of satisfaction blended with his harshly
guttural moan of pleasure. He tried to draw her into a
closer embrace, but was impeded by the console between them. With an unspoken curse aimed at the designer of bucket seats, he drew back his head to look
at her bemused features. His eyes glittered with the
brilliance of emeralds as he reached for a lever near the
door. As his seat slid backward, he lifted Erin across
his lap in a single, smooth motion that left her gasping.

When he pressed her head against the supporting
curve of his arm and raised his hand to undo the knot
in his tie, Erin couldn't speak. She watched the dex-
terous fingers in an agony of suspense, the warmth of
his body an enticement she couldn't resist. Her heart
beat erratically as she looked up at him with open
yearning in her eyes. He held her gaze while he sys-
tematically unfastened his suit jacket, his movements
unhurried and deliberately provocative. "Unbutton
my shirt, Erin."

Logan's deep voice hypnotized her into instant
compliance, and before she was aware of having
moved she was obeying his quietly spoken command.
Her eyes grew wide with intrigue as she waited to un-
cover the male beauty hidden by his shirt, their depths
as luminous as wisps of blue-gray smoke. She felt
clumsy and uncoordinated as she struggled to sepa-

rate buttons from their corresponding holes, her fingers trembling so badly she cried out in frustration. "Help me, Logan."

With an assenting growl he took over the task, pushing aside the edges of his shirt as he tugged the material out of his slacks. Then he lifted her shaking hand to his mouth, his smoldering glance memorizing every line and angle of her face as he bit softly at the flesh between her thumb and forefinger. She gasped as a jolt of electrified sensation sent chills skittering up her spine, her chest rising and falling with alarming rapidity as she struggled to draw oxygen into her lungs.

Erin didn't think it was possible for her breathing to become any more erratic, but she soon learned differently. When Logan pressed her hand against the furry warmth of his chest and reached behind her neck to release the tie on her dress, she stopped breathing entirely. "Logan?" she asked uncertainly.

"Hush, little one," he breathed softly. "There's no one around to see us."

She squirmed uneasily, abruptly stilling her movements when Logan gasped in arousal. Her expression held both desire and trepidation as she protested the extent of the intimacy he was creating between them. "I don't think we should . . ."

"Now's not the time for rational thought," he murmured with an enticing smile. "Aren't you curious, baby? Don't you want to know what it feels like to bury your breasts against me without the barrier of clothes to hamper the pleasure?"

Erin glanced at the dark whorls of hair covering his chest, and swallowed heavily. To feel what he was describing was suddenly her idea of heaven, but years of moral conditioning couldn't be overcome in an instant. For the first time in her life she fully understood the immensely seductive power of desire, her conscience struggling against the raging demands of the flesh.

Logan reached toward the material still covering her breasts, and teasingly flicked his thumb over the hardened outline of a nipple. With a surprised gasp she arched her back, a low moan escaping from her parted lips. Spurred into action by the sound, he bent his head and covered the furiously racing pulse beating against her throat with his hungry mouth. Erin moaned again, on the verge of tears by the shocking pleasure-pain of arousal. Returning his hand to its former position against her neck, he began to lower the bodice of her dress.

"So sweet." He sighed, his tongue capturing the fine sheen of moisture bathing her temple. "You're so honey-sweet, baby. I want to taste every inch of you."

Erin's fingers curled into a fist against his chest, her other arm trapped between his body and her own. She began to push against him, panicking when she realized how helpless she was against his superior strength. "Please, don't . . . don't, Logan."

Her stricken cry pierced the magical world of pleasure enveloping him in a sensual haze. Every muscle in his taut frame clenched as he lifted his head, and noticed the tears flooding her eyes. "Oh, God!"

With remorse replacing his ardor, he whispered, "I've scared you out of your wits, haven't I? I didn't mean to go beyond a few kisses, and especially not in the damn front seat of my car, Erin."

At the self-disgust coloring his voice, laughter mingled with Erin's sobs. Every inch of her small frame was shaking in reaction, and yet her eyes held understanding as she looked up at him. "I know you didn't, Logan. It's not your fault that I'm a repressed idiot. Sometimes I think I must be the only virgin my age left on the face of the earth."

"I'm the one who's behaved like a blasted idiot!" He cradled her protectively, his expression rueful. "I should have remembered how shy you are, and realized that your innocence is more than a technicality."

She frowned in perplexity. "What do you mean by technicality?"

"In the circles I move in women learn the value of virginity at an early age. They aren't about to lose it unless a wedding ring is on their finger, but not through any moral reservations. They're usually willing to do everything else a man might desire, especially if he's rich," he concluded disparagingly. "That makes him a good investment for the future."

Her eyes widened in sudden apprehension. "Logan, you don't think that I . . . ?"

"Of course not!" he muttered gruffly. "How could I, when you're still shaking with unslaked passion? Believe me, those women I mentioned wouldn't have stopped me until I'd satisfied them with my mouth or hands."

A vivid blush stained Erin's cheeks. "I . . . see," she murmured weakly.

Logan felt another tremor slice through her body, and tightened his arms around her. Closing his eyes, he leaned his head against the supple leather of the bucket seat and began to rock her from side to side.

"It passes, sweetheart," he murmured deeply. "Just hold on to me for a minute until the ache goes away."

Another shudder gripped her and she wrapped her arms tightly around his neck. "Is it the same for you?"

He shifted uncomfortably. "Yes, only maybe it hurts a bit more."

She rested her cheek against his chest, and felt the rapid thud of his heartbeats begin to slow into a more natural rhythm. "I didn't mean to hurt you."

The admission made him smile, and his lashes lifted to allow him to view her stricken features. He carefully wiped away the residue of tears from her cheeks, his touch gentle as he gazed down at her. "You mean you didn't know you could," he remarked dryly.

"Not really." She ducked her head with shy evasion, her breath warm against his chest as she sighed. "Books and discussions with my friends hardly prepared me for reality, did it?"

He placed a curved forefinger beneath her chin, forcing her to look at him. "Virgin or not, you haven't reached the age of twenty-three without dating. Surely I'm not the first man who's shown you he wants you?"

"No, but I always avoided dating the others." A dimple popped out beside her mouth as she smiled impishly. "I should have ducked when I saw you coming."

"You certainly should have." His expression intent, he asked, "Why didn't you, Erin?"

"Because you're the first man I've ever wanted."

He gave her a reproving glare and groaned. "Don't you know better than to admit something like that with your clothes still half off?"

Logan jerked up her dress and hurriedly tied it into a firm knot. When she rubbed her cheek against his chest with trusting affection, he stiffened in silent protest at her innocent provocation. Expelling his breath in exasperation, he muttered, "I don't know how in God's name you've kept your virginity this long!"

"I've never been tempted to lose it," she sighed.

He grumbled a warning. "If you keep tempting me, you won't have anything left to lose, sweetheart."

She linked her fingers together behind his neck, and burrowed her face against his throat. "I just didn't think you could be attracted to someone like me."

"What do you mean, someone like you?"

"I'm so ordinary."

He gave a snort of derision and gripped her shoulders, levering her reclining form into a sitting position. "You, my lady, are lovely and quite special. You possess a gentle soul and an unusual degree of honesty, which are rare qualities in this superficial society we live in. What surprises me is that some man hasn't broken through your defenses and convinced you of that before now."

"No one's ever cared enough to try."

"I care," he murmured softly, "but I'm not going to lie to you, Erin. I would be faithful to you while we're lovers. But I've never been much good at lasting relationships, and I probably never will be. Marriage is a silken trap I have no intention of being caught in. I want you more than any woman I've ever known, but I can't promise you hearts-and-flowers and forever. I can only promise to be a tender lover, one unselfish enough to put your needs first.''

Pain sliced through Erin, swift and deadly and agonizing in its intensity. He had distanced himself from her with a few words, and dreams she'd been unaware of harboring shattered around her. "And when it's over?" she asked sadly. "What happens then, Logan?"

"The future will have to take care of itself, but I hope we will always remain friends, Erin."

"My parents certainly never felt trapped by their marriage," she remarked bitterly. "They are as much in love with each other today as they were in the beginning, because they weren't afraid to make a commitment to a future together. They certainly didn't enter into their relationship anticipating its ending. What you want from me goes against everything I've been brought up to believe in, Logan."

"You are more of a rarity than I realized." He was appalled at even considering taking a virgin as his mistress, and shame placed a curt note of sarcasm in his voice. "Your parents are to be congratulated, Erin."

Her teeth began to nibble her bottom lip, but anger showed in the tightness of her jaw. "So my upbringing was sheltered, is there anything wrong with that?"

His guilty conscience growing more acute as each moment passed, he was curtly defensive. "Did I say there was?"

"You implied it!"

"I wasn't criticizing you," he said in exasperation, as he gripped her waist and shifted her into her own seat. "Stating a fact is not making a judgment."

"I happen to believe that making love should mean more than an exchange of goods."

"And you think I don't?"

She flinched at the offended accusation in his voice, but valiantly stood her ground. "Now who's making stupid assumptions?"

Logan was on the verge of telling her to forget the whole thing, until he heard the tremor in her voice and saw the wounded look in her eyes. With a muffled groan he reached out, and cradled her face between his hands. "I'm acting like a petulant child who's been denied a treat, instead of a grown man who's old enough to have learned to be patient. How in the world did this conversation get started?"

Although it was an apology of sorts, Erin was well aware that he hadn't retracted his earlier comments. From what she'd gathered from the few things he'd let slip, his childhood had been appalling. He hadn't grown up with the security she'd known, and his experiences had hardened and disillusioned him. From the things he'd said about his mother, she was a cold, selfish woman. As for his father, she hadn't been deaf to the note of pity in Logan's voice when he'd briefly mentioned him.

If she'd had an upbringing like Logan's, wouldn't she find it impossible to trust anyone with her feelings? Of course she would, but that knowledge didn't solve the problem she was now facing. The real crux of the matter was, would she be able to teach this man to trust in the love she might one day feel for him? She was already halfway to loving him, she realized in dismay, but would she be able to enter his world and become the kind of woman he needed without counting the cost to herself? She didn't know, but with every fiber of her being she knew she had to take her chances.

With a trembling smile she grasped Logan's wrists and turned her head to place a kiss against this open palm. "It doesn't matter how our conversation began," she whispered. "What's really important is that we learn more about each other. You've told me what you expect from an intimate relationship between us, and I have to respect that kind of honesty. I just need more time to come to terms with my own feelings toward you, Logan."

"Don't you think I know that?" he muttered with self-derision. "I feel like the lowest form of life for trying to seduce you, and for your sake I should leave you the hell alone. But I don't think I can, Erin. I can't seem to help myself where you're concerned."

Her eyes glowed, her voice soft with tenderness. "Then that makes two of us. Will knowing that I don't want you to leave me alone ease your guilt?"

"Damn it, there you go again, saying things that make me hotter than hell," he muttered through gritted teeth. "You're the most exasperating female I've ever met!"

Her rounded chin tilted defiantly. "Why shouldn't I be as honest with you as you've been with me? I may not be very experienced, but even I know that lovemaking is a team effort."

His brows tipped roguishly. "As in orgy?"

Laughing, she punched his shoulder. "As in you and me together, you wicked man."

His features sobered abruptly. "Compared to you I *am* wicked, sweetheart. I've been around the block quite a few times, and you haven't even crossed the street. Physically we react explosively to each other, and it would be easy for me to seduce you into thinking my way. But if we become lovers, I don't want it to be because you were blinded by desire, Erin."

He gave a cynical laugh, his thumbs gently brushing her soft cheeks. Pressing his lips to her forehead, he remarked, "Once you know me better, you might not even like me much."

"I'm not worried," she confided with certainty. "I only hope you don't end up disappointed in me."

"Never," he whispered fervently. "You could never disappoint me, Erin."

Erin was glad Logan had a meeting to attend the next morning, since she wasn't exactly at her best. She had tossed and turned for hours last night, her mind in a turmoil as she went over and over every moment they'd spent together. Pieces of remembered conversation played havoc with her concentration, and she could feel a headache beginning to throb against her temples as she sat hunched over her desk.

"Well, you're certainly something of a dark horse," said a sneering voice from the doorway.

Erin's head jerked up, her attention caught by the malevolent gleam in Lorna Phelps's obsidian eyes. "I beg your pardon?" she questioned tautly.

"You certainly should, and don't bother pretending you don't know what I'm talking about. You might have Logan fooled by those big blue eyes of yours, but I'm not suckered by your sweet-little-girl act.''

''Since I really don't know what in the world you mean, I suggest you leave my office, Lorna. I've got work to do, even if you haven't.''

''Logan is mine,'' Lorna hissed. ''His mother and I are already planning the wedding.''

''Then don't you think you should tell Logan?''

Lorna's harsh laughter filled the room. ''He's well aware of his mother's expectations, and just as aware of his duty to his family name. Don't be blinded by his expertise as a lover into thinking he'll ever marry someone socially unacceptable.''

Erin's eyes flashed. ''Someone like me?''

''You said it, darling. You're nothing more than a temporary diversion, and one of many at that,'' the other woman concluded nastily. ''Logan is a very highly sexed man. Since I'm not willing to satisfy his baser needs until we're married, he naturally has his little flings.''

Remembering Logan's disdain for women who bartered sex for a wedding ring, Erin just smiled. ''Thank you for the warning, but I prefer to trust in Logan's integrity.''

Enraged by Erin's derogatory amusement, Lorna's eyelids narrowed into furious slits. There was hatred in her voice as she taunted, ''Such a goody-goody. I don't know how you can look so innocent after your romp with Logan last night.''

Erin's features whitened and her stomach lurched sickeningly. ''What do you know about last night?''

Lorna gave her a look of wide-eyed innocence. "Only what I read on the card."

Ready to scream with impatience, Erin counted to ten before she spoke. "What card?"

"Why, the one that came with the flowers waiting on my desk for you."

"You had no right reading a personal note intended for me!"

Lorna buffed her nails against her blouse and gave Erin a look of contempt. "Of course, I feel Logan was overly generous. Two dozen red roses is too romantic a gesture to make for a mere one-night stand. It might give you the wrong idea."

"You're the one with the wrong ideas," Erin snapped angrily. "I hope you're satisfied with the results of your snooping."

Draping her slim, silk-clad body against the door frame, Lorna's eyes flashed with derision. "It's Logan you should hope to keep satisfied, but you don't have a prayer. He'll soon get tired of your overblown charms and see you for the low-class slut you are."

With an outraged gasp Erin jumped to her feet, her entire body shaking as she defended herself against the other woman's vicious attack. "I think you've said enough!"

"It will do for now," Lorna drawled smugly as she turned to leave. "By the way, I suggest you collect your sexual tribute before I stuff it down the toilet."

Five

After the dreadful scene with Lorna, Erin found it difficult to behave as though nothing had happened. She had placed Logan's beautiful floral arrangement on the corner of her desk, wincing when she read his note thanking her for a lovely evening. Although she appreciated his thoughtfulness, she felt sick remembering that Lorna had read the note and handled the flowers. She was still preoccupied when she met Carrie for lunch, and her new friend was quick to notice her depressed mood. "What's wrong, Erin?" she asked in concern.

Erin quickly related the details of her confrontation with Lorna, and shook her head in perplexity. "Logan has dated a lot of women, Carrie. I can't understand why Lorna has singled me out for a hate campaign."

"I don't see what there is to understand," Carrie stated with a derisively explicit sniff. "The Dragon Lady is as jealous as hell of you, Erin."

"But she started in on me before I was even interviewed by Logan."

"That's because she took one look at you and knew you'd be heavy competition for her. You're far prettier and smarter than she is, and a heck of a lot nicer than she could ever hope to be."

Erin's compassionate heart smote her. "It must be terrible to love a man to the point of obsession, especially when he doesn't return your affection."

"Don't you go feeling sorry for her," Carrie retorted. "It's my confirmed opinion that our Lorna is too wrapped up in herself to feel love for anyone else. But as you found out this morning, she's made up her mind to become Mrs. Logan Sinclair and nothing's going to change it."

Haltingly Erin repeated what Lorna had told her. "According to her, she and Logan's mother are already planning their wedding."

"I wouldn't doubt it," Carrie said disparagingly. "Lorna is just the kind of daughter-in-law Mrs. Sinclair would favor, which isn't surprising since those two have been fashioned from the same mold. I imagine Logan's godmother is much the same."

Erin was puzzled by this latest reference. "What does his godmother have to do with anything?"

Carrie's brows rose in an incredulous arc. "Didn't Lorna see fit to inform you of her exalted position in the Sinclair household?"

Erin's brow rose in consternation. "I didn't know she and Logan were related."

Carrie nibbled a piece of turkey from the salad in front of her with a contemplative air. "She'd like to think she is. Apparently her mother and Logan's are the best of friends. They attended the same private schools as girls, were launched into society at the same debutante ball, and each stands as godmother to the other's child."

Carrie stabbed at a piece of tomato with more force than accuracy. "It's my guess that a little familial pressure was put on the boss to hire Lorna. Originally she was supposed to be the one to replace his secretary, but luckily for me she didn't know beans about the job. So Logan dumped her at the reception desk, where all she has to do is look glamorous and answer the phone."

"I see," Erin murmured. "At least, I think I do. But if she comes from that kind of privileged background, why is she working at all?"

"So she can bird-dog Logan, why else?"

"You've got a point," Erin laughed wryly.

Carrie pushed her meal aside and leaned across the table, her eyes shadowed with apprehension. "Watch out for her, Erin. She's already trying to spread rumors about you and Logan, not that anybody is paying any attention. I'm not the only one around here who has her number."

"What kind of rumors?" Erin asked in clipped accents, though she had already made an educated guess.

Carrie flushed with embarrassment. "She's saying Logan only hired you because you were already his mistress, which we all know is a crock."

"Mud sticks, Carrie." Erin's expression conveyed her distress, and she gave a despondent shake of her head. "The trouble is, Logan and I *are* attracted to each other. This kind of gossip could destroy our relationship before it even has a chance to get started. I can't risk ruining his reputation with his staff."

"How could the two of you falling in love do that?" the other woman demanded forcefully. "Logan's a good guy, and we'd all like to see him happy. Lorna's a nasty piece of work, but surely you can keep an eagle eye on her without letting her interfere. Just keep in mind that she's sly and manipulative, and remember to cover your back. She's likely to pull out all the stops where you're concerned, and I wouldn't be surprised if she has a few tricks up her sleeve."

Erin shook her head despondently. "Why can't life be simple?"

Carrie gave a trill of laughter and wrinkled her pert nose. "Because we'd probably die of boredom."

"Boredom I can handle," Erin rejoined bitterly. "It's this kind of jealous intrigue I have trouble dealing with."

"That's because you haven't got an ounce of nastiness in your entire body, unlike me. If I wasn't worried about you I'd be relishing this entire situation. Lorna's especially livid at the idea of you traveling with the boss, which is tickling the daylights out of me and everyone else around here. Heaven knows she's lorded it over the rest of us long enough. It's about time she was put in her place."

Startled, Erin asked, "How do you know she's upset about Logan and me traveling together?"

"I just happened to overhear a call she made to Logan's mother," Carrie admitted without a trace of shame for eavesdropping on a private conversation.

Her eyebrows lifted and fell with comic regularity, and her mouth parted on an impish grin. "It was extremely edifying."

"But overseeing his other clubs is a part of my job," Erin exclaimed with an exasperated grimace. "What does she imagine I should do, refuse to accompany him?"

"Just keep your eyes and ears open," Carrie pleaded with a return to her earlier seriousness. "As far as Lorna Phelps is concerned you pose a threat, one she's going to do her best to eliminate. I don't want to see you get hurt, Erin."

As Erin parted from her friend to return to her office, Carrie's warnings went around and around in her head. She was disturbed to think that Logan had hired Lorna to keep the peace in his family, and couldn't help wondering if Mrs. Sinclair had more influence over him than he realized. Her relationship with her son might be distant, but she was still his mother.

There was so much she and Logan needed to learn about each other, their attraction new and very fragile. Could it withstand his family's opposition, especially since the differences between them seemed an insurmountable barrier to any happiness they might find together? Erin drew in a ragged breath, and scolded herself for anticipating trouble. After all, why worry about a relationship which might never materialize?

But she couldn't seem to prevent herself from longing for those hearts and flowers Logan had mentioned, she realized despairingly. When she remembered that he wanted nothing more from her than a temporary liaison, she wondered how she could be so stupid. Wouldn't she be better off distancing herself from him now, before she ended up getting her heart broken? The questions seemed endless, and she couldn't produce any answers.

There was only one thing of which she was certain. She wasn't elegant, sophisticated or experienced in the ways of the world, and she didn't even know if she wanted to be. If Lorna Phelps was any example of the upper crust of society, she would gladly give it a miss. *But last night you realized just how vulnerable you are to Logan,* an inner voice taunted. *What if your attraction to him grows into love? Won't you want to fit into his background and be the kind of woman he can be proud of?*

Erin didn't have to deliberate long over the answer, and as she considered the uncertain future a pensive frown creased her brows. Logan expected to be far enough along with their screening project in a month or so to begin their training program. From that point on they would be travelling together a good deal of the time and forced into close proximity. Remembering the swiftly overpowering arousal she'd experienced in his arms, she didn't have much confidence in being able to hold out if he decided to make love to her. Indeed she wasn't even certain she wanted to deny the sensual appeal he held for her.

As if that wasn't enough to cause her countless sleepless hours, Erin was also disturbed at the possibility of letting him down in a professional capacity. There would be meetings not only with members of his staff, but he had also mentioned hosting a small get-together to introduce her to his board of directors and several of his closest friends. They were people from

his environment, and she was worried about the kind
of impression she would make on them. Would they
be as critical and disdainful of her as Lorna had been?

No, they damn well wouldn't! she decided with a
determined toss of her head. She was now making an
excellent salary, and she knew exactly how most of her
first check was going to be spent. By the time the night
of the party arrived, she was going to look as sleek and
self-confident as any woman there if it killed her!
Linda had a flair for fashion, and would delight in
dragging her through the malls in search of a more
suitable wardrobe. Her friend had been itching to
make her over for years and at the prospect of endless
hours of scouring dress and lingerie shops, Erin
wished she had a pillow under which to hide her head.

Logan's idea of a small get-together and her own
vastly differed, as she realized the moment she scanned
the nearly full parking lot of the restaurant in Jack
London Square he had reserved for this evening's fes-
tivities. Logan had wanted her to accompany him to
the party, but she had insisted on driving herself. As
host he needed to be the first to arrive and the last to
leave, while she was hoping to avert a nervous break-
down by barely arriving on time and making an early
escape.

Parking her squat, dented Volkswagen between a
gleaming Mercedes and an impressively long Caddy
didn't do much to raise her confidence. But as she slid
from her car and felt her new silk-jersey evening gown
brush over her legs, she found her spirits lifting. The
rose-colored creation was a designer model that although marked down by nearly half had still cost more

than she usually spent on clothes in a year. But once she had tried it on in the fitting room, she hadn't been able to resist its purchase. It was a dream of a dress, and she knew its simple, understated design suited her.

As she entered the restaurant, her eyes darted nervously around the room and instantly approved the subdued elegance of her surroundings. The ceiling was peaked and interspersed with dark wooden beams, and brass and silver lamps were affixed to highly polished sheets of intricately grained wall paneling. Round tables draped with white linen cloths covered two-thirds of the room, the other third taken up by a dance floor. A mirrored wall behind a curved bar reflected the dancers, the men distinguished in formal attire and the women as colorful as a bevy of fluttering butterflies.

Erin suddenly felt like Cinderella ready to attend the ball. She tingled with nervous anticipation, and to add to the fantasy she saw her Prince Charming approaching her through the crowd. In casual attire Logan was impressive, but in a black tuxedo he was devastating. His shoulders appeared broader, his waist and hips leaner, his height even more pronounced. Her mouth went dry as he paused in front of her, his eyes holding a slumberous sensuality as they wandered over her tensely held figure.

"You've outdone yourself, Erin," he admitted huskily. "Tonight you're not just beautiful, you're absolutely exquisite."

Her eyes seemed trapped within the glowing depths of his, the intimacy of the moment not lessened by the people around them. "Thank you," she finally managed to say. "I wasn't certain my dress would be suitable for the occasion."

"I only have one complaint about that silken bit of witchery." He lowered his head, his warm lips brushing against her ear as he murmured, "I'm going to spend most of the night jealous of every man who comes near you."

She caught her breath and flushed with pleasure. "You're just fishing for a compliment," she said with a shaken laugh. "You know you're the handsomest man here."

Logan's features softened with tenderness at the artlessness of her response. "I'm glad you think so, but when you say things like that you make it damned hard for me to keep my hands off you."

Erin lowered her gaze to his ruffled white shirtfront. Since their night out Logan's manner toward her had been friendly but impersonal, and she'd agonized about the reason for his changed attitude. He delighted in teasing her much the way a brother would, but instead of being relieved by a lessening of his ardor she'd been dismayed at the extent of her disappointment. She'd had a taste of his lovemaking, and it had left her hungry for more.

"I've...wondered about that," she whispered. "You've seemed very distant lately."

"Because I avoid touching you; being alone with you?" he asked quietly. "It's self-defense, Erin."

"Why should you need to defend yourself against me? Unless...unless you've changed your mind about your feelings." She angled her head proudly, but there was a slight quiver to her mouth as she told him, "It's all right. I do understand, Logan. We just got carried away by the moonlight, but I never really took you seriously when you said you wanted me."

Her lashes lifted to reveal the pain she was trying so hard to conceal, and Logan winced inwardly. Dear God! he thought in a near frenzy of frustration. Didn't she realize he'd kept his distance to protect her from the desire he felt every time she came near him? He remembered how often he had longed to pull her into his arms and to stifle any protests she might make with the hungry urgency of his mouth, and here she was telling him she'd never taken him seriously!

When he thought of all the nights he'd spent imagining her beside him in the darkness, his body in a fever of need for her, he didn't know whether to shake her to her senses or to drag her off to his bed. He knew which solution appealed to him more, but heaven help him, he was trying to give her time to come to terms with her own feelings! She certainly wasn't making it easy for him, and at the moment his patience was wearing pretty thin.

Evidence of this was in his voice as he muttered a harsh expletive and grabbed her hand. Startled by his abruptness, she cried out as he dragged her across the room. "Where are you taking me?"

"I want to dance with you."

When they reached the crowded dance floor he drew her into his arms, his mouth compressed into a tight, angry line as he rasped, "So you never took me seriously, did you?"

Bewildered by his explosive mood, Erin resisted the closeness of his embrace. His body was pressed to hers, their thighs brushing as he swayed her in time to the sensuous melody being played by the band. She shivered as his hands wandered slowly over her back, her eyes closing at the exquisite sensations aroused by his touch. "Logan, I . . ."

He lowered his hands until they were pressing against the base of her spine, his voice gruff as he asked, "Can you feel what's happening to me, baby? Do you still think I don't want you?"

Her hands slid from his shoulders to link around his neck, and her body melted against him with undisguised satisfaction. "Should I be shocked?"

He gave a rueful laugh and brushed his mouth against her temple. "You never cease to surprise me, woman. I'm seducing you on the dance floor, and instead of reacting like any other self-respecting virgin you're encouraging me."

"Mmm, is that what I'm doing?"

Erin stood on her tiptoes and arched her back. Logan was unable to suppress a shudder as her hips cradled his hardened masculinity. "Show a little mercy, Erin!"

She allowed him to place some breathing room between them, but her mouth formed a protesting pout. "I'm not in the mood to be merciful."

"What are you in the mood for?" he questioned throatily.

Erin's lips curved into an unconsciously seductive smile, as she whispered, "I think you know."

Logan's eyes closed on a muffled groan. "You are sorely straining my willpower, you little tease."

"And if I'm not teasing?" she asked, stiffening in his embrace as she waited for his reply.

It was immediately forthcoming, but was definitely not what she had hoped to hear. "Then we have a hellish few weeks ahead of us, Erin." He opened his eyes, the expression in their depths one of brooding sternness. "Might I remind you that you were the one who said she needed more time to sort out her feelings? I agreed to give you that time, and I'm not going back on my decision."

Erin couldn't believe her own boldness as she gently brushed her fingers against the back of his neck, her body once again inclining toward his. She felt no shyness or hesitation with this man, because with Logan flirting seemed to come naturally. "You are a very stubborn man," she said with a disgruntled sigh, "and I don't need anymore time to know how I feel about you."

"Nevertheless, taking your first lover will be a big step for you," he remarked heavily. "Maybe I'm the one who needs more time, honey. I want you desperately, but I'm not callous enough to put my welfare above your own. I have to be absolutely certain you know what you're getting into."

Erin pressed her forehead against the shiny lapel of his jacket, his reference to being her first lover ringing in her ears. "I won't ever want any other man but you, Logan," she mumbled in choked accents. "How could you even suggest such a thing?"

His hand cradled her jaw as he tilted her head back to study her distressed features. His smile held a wealth of sadness, and his voice was gruff with suppressed emotion. "You're so young and idealistic you frighten me. I should be shot for even contemplating a love affair with you."

"You certainly don't think of me as a child, so why treat me like one, Logan? Possibly you *are* the one who needs more time to know what you want, be-

cause if you object to my idealistic attitude toward life
and the future, then maybe I'm not the right woman
for you, after all.''

The music had drawn to a conclusion, and as she
spoke Erin started to turn away from him. But when
she would have departed the dance floor, a firm hand
on her arm stopped her. ''You are the right woman,''
he conceded harshly, ''but more importantly you're
the only one I want.'' His eyes glittered against the
sudden pallor of his face. ''Don't condemn me for
looking out for your welfare, Erin. I couldn't live with
myself if I ever hurt you.''

Logan's pained admission left her feeling almost
lightheaded with relief as he guided her off the floor.
He might not be in love with her, but he cared about
her very much. Given time and patience, he might one
day trust in her enough to consider a future together.
That he also might not didn't bear thinking about.
Shaking off the threat of depression, she slanted him
a teasing smile. ''You can look out for me all you like,
but don't count on my cooperation, Logan. I'll go
along with your decision to wait up to a point, but beyond that I can't promise not to seduce you.''

''You little wretch,'' he said with a laugh. ''I'd better introduce you to everyone before you decide to
turn on any more heat. I don't think my aging heart
can stand the strain.''

''Then lead on, oh venerable one,'' she responded
pertly.

Logan circled her waist and began to urge her forward, but was halted by a hand clutching his sleeve.
''You won't leave me?'' a small voice enquired with
timid anxiety.

He stared into eyes which had lost every trace of self-confidence, and responded to her sudden apprehension with a gentle smile. "I won't leave you," he promised quietly, "but you have nothing to worry about. Everyone is going to love you, honey."

Then why can't you? she thought as he led her across the room. Why can't you, Logan?

The next few weeks passed swiftly for Erin. She was working harder than she'd ever worked before and was, quite frankly, having the time of her life. Gradually she became acquainted with the rest of the staff, and she found them to be a fairly outgoing and gregarious group. Their camaraderie was infectious, and made her feel as though she belonged. When she was asked her opinion of a new fad diet going the rounds, she knew she'd been accepted professionally as well as personally.

Unfortunately her relationship with Logan wasn't so simple to analyze. They seemed to have reached a stalemate, no closer and no farther apart than they'd been the night of the party. She was treated to his caustic wit and devilish sense of humor on a daily basis, until she'd finally learned to give as good as she got. When she even began to engineer some of their verbal sparring matches, he seemed inordinately pleased by her growing self-assurance.

Just this morning she'd managed to get some of her own back, and at the memory she uttered a quietly amused laugh. Logan had been crouched beside the pool, showing her how to clean the filter and add chemicals to the water when a young, precocious and extremely spoiled teenager spotted him. The girl rushed out of the sauna and accidentally on purpose dropped her towel at his feet.

Erin had nearly died with embarrassment, but to Logan's credit he remained impervious to the girl's nakedness. With an impassive expression on his face he picked up the towel and handed it back to that bold little madam with a sardonically amused smile. Chagrined at having her natural attributes ignored, the girl flounced off with a sulky face and goose bumps.

Not one to let such a perfect opportunity pass her by, when Logan straightened Erin gave him a demurely sympathetic look and a consoling pat on his arm. Leaning against him, she murmured, "Poor man, how upsetting for you."

His eyes instantly narrowed in suspicion. "I'm not upset," he stated flatly. "She's just a kid showing off, trying to draw attention to herself."

Giving her best rendition of a soulful glance, she slowly moistened her lips with the tip of her tongue. "But it must be terrible for you."

Logan's throat convulsed as he swallowed, a slightly dazed look in his eyes as he unblinkingly followed the movement of her tongue. "What must be terrible?"

Bracing herself against his side, she stretched to her full height and whispered in his ear. "Why, having women lusting after that magnificent body of yours, of course. You must hate being viewed as a walking sex object."

When she saw the mottled color creep up his neck, she'd had difficulty keeping herself from howling with laughter. Only the sweetness of revenge kept a smile from spreading all over her face, and she quickly lowered her head to prevent him from seeing the triumph glittering in her eyes. If eyes were really mirrors of the soul, she thought humorously, she was going to have a tough time with the man upstairs.

But as it turned out she shouldn't have been so ready to congratulate herself for turning the tables on the dratted man, since his husky voice brought her head up in a flash. "You don't know how badly I've wanted to hear you admit that, Erin."

She eyed him warily, confused by the odd look on his face. "What did I say?"

His grin was pure, unadulterated sorcery, his emerald eyes flashing a signal that sizzled her brain. "That you're lusting after my body."

Too late, she realized she should have taken into account that incisive mind of his and run like hell. Instead she stood gaping at him stupidly, her apprehension increasing as his glance slid over her with sensual expertise. "I never!" she lied without the least compunction.

"Then why would you think of me as a magnificent sex object?"

"A walking sex object," she corrected indignantly.

The corner of his mouth twitched betrayingly as he took a step in her direction. "With a magnificent body."

"Don't press your luck."

Logan continued to move forward, determination in his steady gaze. Erin backed away from his stalking figure, one hand raised as if to protect herself from any sudden moves. "Now Logan, forgiveness is next to godliness."

His deep-throated laughter did a tap dance along her spinal column. "That's cleanliness, and I'm not ready to forgive you yet, sweetheart."

With a panicky glance over her shoulder, she realized how close she was to the edge of the pool. This situation was beginning to call for drastic measures, she decided frantically. Quickly sidestepping to reverse their positions, she muttered, "You want clean, I'll give you clean!"

Logan made a very satisfactory splash as he hit the water and surfaced spluttering. Immediately his strong arms began to propel him in her direction, but she wasn't stupid enough to wait around to hear what he had to say. Although she told herself it was common sense and not cowardliness that lent her running feet an extra burst of speed, she had quite prudently avoided being alone with him ever since. During the course of the day their paths had inevitably crossed, but so far he hadn't had a chance to retaliate. Yet if the vengeful gleam in his eyes whenever he spotted her was any indication, she knew she was in for a world of trouble.

Stretching tiredly, Erin glanced at the clock on the wall and winced. She'd locked up nearly an hour and a half ago, and here she was still hunched over her desk at ten-thirty at night. Logan would have a fit if he knew she was working this late, but he'd had a city-council meeting to attend and had left early for a change. Fortunately for her, she decided with a grin. His absence had saved her from having to spend any more time dodging him.

A wide yawn caught her by surprise, and with a muffled groan she pushed back her chair and rose to her feet. As she bent down to get her canvas shoulder bag from the bottom drawer of her desk, the muscles in her neck protested painfully. She usually spent part of her lunch hour working out, and she'd obviously done so a mite too strenuously this afternoon. Added to that, she'd foregone her usual stint in the sauna, choosing instead to complete some questionnaires she would need this weekend.

She and Logan were leaving for Sacramento in the morning, and she needed to have these forms available for the conference they were organizing. Logan had decided to give a series of seminars prior to visiting his individual clubs to provide hands-on training, and Citrus Heights in Sacramento was the last on their list. If she didn't get home soon she was going to be dead from lack of sleep tomorrow, but after a brief moment of hesitation she decided to forget the lateness of the hour and head for the sauna. A few more minutes one way or the other wasn't going to matter, but driving to Sacramento with a crick in her neck certainly was.

Slipping the completed forms into her briefcase, Erin locked the office behind her and skirted the dimly lighted lobby. As she passed the reception desk she grimaced. If there was one worm in her apple, she thought with irritation, it was Lorna Phelps. The other woman lost no opportunity to glare at her or to mutter disparaging remarks. Of course she was cunning enough to do so beneath her breath or when Logan was out of earshot.

Her sneaky viciousness set Erin on edge, but there wasn't much she could do about it. Since she wasn't working directly with Lorna she was usually able to ignore the sly digs aimed at undermining her self-confidence, and at least the gossip she'd instigated had ceased. She had a hunch Logan was responsible for the latter, and if that was the case it would be just one more blot on her copybook where the Dragon Lady was concerned.

Erin swiftly guided her thoughts in a more pleasant direction. She was looking forward to the coming weekend. The first two conferences she and Logan had organized had gone well, and after this one was concluded they would be heading for Monterey. One of Logan's largest clubs was located there, and he had decided it would be a perfect place to start their actual training program. For entirely selfish reasons she also thought it would be perfect. She loved the beaches and the quaint shops and restaurants along Cannery Row, which had gained historical significance through the work of famed author John Steinbeck.

Upon reaching the dressing rooms, Erin stripped off her clothes and wrapped a large, fluffy white towel sarong-fashion around herself. Since she was alone she didn't bother with a bathing suit. Leaving her belongings on one of the padded benches in front of the locker area, she hurried toward the sauna. Her nakedness beneath the towel made her feel positively wicked, and her mouth widened in a grin. This job was definitely causing some changes in Ms. Erin Daniels, she decided with a laugh. If she wasn't careful, she might just end up an extrovert!

Logan pulled into the parking lot and scowled when he spotted Linda's motorcycle, which she'd loaned to Erin while her car was in the shop for repairs. What the devil was Erin still doing here? he wondered with irritation. She knew he worried about her riding around on that thing this late at night. Yes, but the obstinate woman had a mind of her own and a perverse nature to go along with it.

Although their working relationship was proving to be excellent, their personal one was the pits. It wasn't her fault he treated her like a pal, but he wanted Erin to view their relationship with a clear, logical mind. The only trouble was, she refused to cooperate. Since the night of the party she'd become increasingly provocative in her manner toward him, and he was becoming damned frustrated.

To add to his troubles, he was beginning to sense a touch of hero worship in Erin's attitude. How was a man supposed to handle a situation like that, when all he wanted to do was to handle the woman doing the worshipping? Uttering a disgusted curse, he exited the car with a scowl on his face. Slamming the door shut, his footsteps crunched on the gravel as he strode toward the club's side entrance.

"Good evening, Mr. Sinclair."

Startled, Logan whirled around and searched for the man that went with the voice. A figure stepped from the shadows, and Logan grinned as he recognized one of his guards. "Hello, Frank. How's it going?"

"Everything's nice and quiet," the elderly man responded.

Logan punched in the code that would turn off the alarm system. "Where's Ted, checking things out inside?"

"No, he's patrolling the grounds. I thought I'd wait to escort Ms. Daniels to the parking lot. This area's pretty secluded, and a woman can't be too careful."

Logan unlocked the door and passed through the entrance. "I appreciate your concern, but I'll see to Ms. Daniels now. You go and join Ted, but would you do me a favor first and lock the Honda in the storage shed? I'll be driving her home tonight."

"I'm real glad of that, Mr. Sinclair. It's just not safe, her haring about after dark on that machine." He was still muttering as he shuffled off. "No, sir. It just ain't safe."

No it wasn't, Logan thought, as she was going to be informed very shortly. Heading toward her office, he realized he was in the mood for a good argument. With any luck she might even yell back at him. He could certainly think of an enjoyable way of shutting her up! His pace increased as he went in search of trouble, the light of battle in his eyes.

Six

____

Erin had poured too much water on the heating elements, and white, billowing puffs of steam filled the sauna. She could barely see her hand in front of her face, not that it made much difference. There was certainly no furniture to fall over, the only obstructions in the box-like, cedar- and redwood-slatted room being the rows of wooden bleachers along the back wall.

She was already perspiring, moisture slipping from her pores in a cleansing flow. Tilting her head back she inhaled deeply, enjoying the pungent scent of cedarwood as it intermingled with the damp air. The radiator hissed enthusiastically as she turned to carefully make her way across the floor, the single, bare light bulb set high in the ceiling casting an eerie glow on her surroundings.

Having reached the mist-enshrouded bleachers, she stretched out on her stomach on the lowest level. The heat would be too intense higher up, and she wriggled around for a moment trying to get comfortable. The towel she'd wrapped around her like a sarong was inching up the back of her thighs, and the knot she'd formed over her breasts was digging into her. She should have taken the darned thing off and spread it over the hard bench, but she wasn't comfortable at the idea of lying about stark naked. Grinning, she decided she wasn't quite as extroverted as she'd thought.

Within minutes the tension began to ooze from her muscles and she sighed with pleasure. Closing her eyes, she let herself drift on a cloud of enjoyable sensation. An unexpected yawn caught her by surprise, and she burrowed her head into a more comfortable position on her crossed arms. A slight frown appeared between her brows. It wasn't wise to allow herself to become too relaxed, she reminded herself, even at this lower level. A sauna raised body temperature fairly rapidly, and she shouldn't stay in here more than ten or fifteen minutes.

She really should open her eyes, she decided drowsily, but she couldn't seem to gather together enough energy to do so. The lumpy towel was no longer digging into her chest, and her body felt as loose and flowing as melted butter. Unsuccessfully muffling another yawn by trying to keep her teeth clenched together, she estimated she'd been lying here for nearly five minutes already. If only she wasn't so sleepy...

Logan entered the pool area, trying to subdue his impatience as his long-legged stride carried him past the furiously rushing waters of the Jacuzzi. Since it was always shut down for the night, he immediately realized his search for Erin had ended. He glanced around the entire area to no avail, but he knew she had to be here somewhere. She was the only one who could have switched the hot tub back on again.

A slow grin creased his mouth as he listened to the sound of the frothing bubbles, his gaze spearing the distance between himself and the small wooden enclosure across the room. A satisfied murmur escaped him when he noticed the red light glowing over the closed door. His quarry wasn't in sight, but it didn't take a genius to determine where his timid little mouse had decided to hole up.

Timid, hah! he thought as his eyes skimmed the placid surface of the swimming pool. There wasn't anything timid about that woman when she decided to be contrary, he could testify to that! Who would have ever suspected that the shy, demure young woman he'd first met was capable of the kind of sexy come-ons she'd been teasing him with these past few weeks? He certainly wouldn't have, but she had outdone herself this morning. The old saying "where there's smoke there's fire" had proven applicable in her case, and even more so in his own. She'd certainly stirred his embers into a blaze without half trying.

When she had leaned into him and breathed hotly into his ear, every muscle in his body, especially those primarily equated with a healthy male, had hardened in reaction. And when she'd whispered to him in that deliberately sultry alto, his heart had pounded against the wall of his chest with such force he thought he was going to be injured for life.

He had almost been relieved when she pushed him into the pool, he recalled with a wry grimace. If she hadn't, he would have given quite a few of his patrons a demonstration of lustful behavior they wouldn't have forgotten in a hurry. His arousal had been swift and sure and stomach-clenching, and he hadn't been in the mood to remember words such as dignity and self-control. Hell, at the time he'd had enough trouble just remembering how to swim!

Already inwardly shaken by that teenage Cleopatra's unveiling, Erin had taken advantage of his discomfiture to take him by surprise. He certainly owed her one, he decided with sardonic righteousness, and she had unwittingly provided him with the perfect opportunity. Uttering a husky laugh, he stared at the closed door of the sauna. It seemed his foolhardy mouse had arranged her own cheese for bait, and all he had to do was spring the trap. Spinning on his heel, he quickly disappeared into one of the changing rooms.

A tiny frown line appeared between Erin's brows as she felt cool air waft across her shoulders and the back of her thighs. She shifted her legs restlessly. She was blissfully comfortable, and the slight chill she felt wasn't enough of an inducement to unglue her eyelids. Then sound blended with sensation, and she jerked upright with a disconcerted gasp. "What are you doing here?"

Logan's eyes wandered over her towel-clad frame with appreciative masculine single-mindedness. "Looking for you."

Erin blinked to clear her sleep-fogged eyes, and immediately wished she hadn't. Now that she could see properly, she was certainly getting an eyeful. Her tongue stuck itself to the roof of her mouth as she stared at Logan. Heavens, he was gorgeous! Clothed the man was attractive, but with only a simple towel between him and complete nudity he was absolutely incredible.

Her stunned gaze rose to inspect his features, and she froze at the expression on his face. He was obviously all too aware of the effect he was having on her, and it was clearly apparent that the knowledge amused him. Well, she didn't find it so damned hilarious. She'd often been ill at ease around the opposite sex, but this was bordering on ridiculous!

Narrowing her eyes in concentration, she desperately gathered together the threads of their conversation. "You had to strip before you started searching?" she demanded with what she hoped was cool disdain.

A rich, mellow chuckle followed the accusation. Moving closer, he crossed his arms over his bare chest and spread his legs until they formed a bracing, inverted vee. She hastily tore her gaze from the bunched muscles of his thighs, barely able to comprehend the meaning behind his words as he said, "I didn't think you'd mind sharing the sauna."

At least he hadn't wanted to share her towel, she thought a touch hysterically. Gesturing toward the farthest end of the bench, she mumbled, "Be my guest."

Erin tried to avert her eyes from Logan, but they didn't seem willing to follow the dictates of her brain. Instead of maintaining a safe distance from his body, they were now riveted on his chest in fascination. His bulging pectorals, covered by a silken spread of body hair, were works of art. The sweat-glistening strands were slightly darker than the hair on his head, and she longed to run her fingers through the luxuriously curly mat. She wondered if the hair on his long, muscular legs would be more abrasive than that on his chest, and could just imagine how they would feel against her own smoothly shaven limbs.

Shaken by the extent of her curiosity, she rushed into awkward speech. "It's time I was leaving, anyway."

Logan's voice was a honey drawl, his eyes positively wicked. "Surely you can take the heat a little longer, or did I gain the wrong impression this morning?"

Erin instantly knew her Waterloo was at hand, and she searched the small enclosure for a means of escape. She had to accept the fact that the only possible exit was the door, which was successfully blocked by one very large, extremely intimidating male personage. She licked the salty moisture from her upper lip and laughed nervously. "Now Logan, you're not going to hold a grudge, are you? You wouldn't be so petty, so small-minded, so..."

"So bent on revenge?" he concluded.

Her eyes widened with apprehension, and she clutched the knot in her towel with both hands. "Uh, aren't you taking this morning's little encounter a touch too seriously?"

He took another step toward her, his voice almost pleasant. "I don't think so."

Erin gave him a conciliatory smile as she scooted closer to the far wall. For a crazy instant she contemplated storming the bleachers, but knew she wouldn't stand a chance if Logan decided to come after her. Not that he'd have to bother chasing her. Another few minutes in this hotbox, especially at a higher elevation, and she would probably turn into a puddle and obligingly drip all over his feet.

"I know I shouldn't have pushed you into the pool," she confessed in barely audible tones, "but I didn't stop to think. It seemed a good idea at the time."

"No, you didn't think," he agreed with a taunting smile, "and I'm not going to, either."

"You're going to throw me in the pool?" Her features mirrored the relief she felt at the thought of escaping with such a mild form of retaliation.

But Logan didn't let her remain complacent for long. Now the smile he sent her way held a sardonic curl, and his words were edged with unmistakable sarcasm. "Something like that."

"Exactly wha-what are you planning to do?"

The tremor in her voice pleased him immensely, and he wasted no more time getting his point across. Joining her on the bench, he wrapped his arm around her shoulders. "I'm going to surrender."

Erin perked up at the admission. "Surrender?"

"Mmm," he murmured with a slight nod of his head. "I've decided to give you what you want."

"What I want?" she squeaked, disgusted by her similarity to a parrot.

"You've managed to seduce me, honey."

She scowled at him. "I have not!"

"Oh, but you have," he whispered huskily. "Why don't I show you?"

Before she had a chance to jerk herself out of his arms, Logan twisted from the waist and lifted her across his lap. The maneuver was accomplished with such swift ease Erin didn't even have time to suck in her breath on a gasp. She stared at the face above her in consternation, her lashes lowering with instinctive defensiveness when he tenderly brushed aside a moistly clinging tendril of hair which clung to her cheek.

Logan stifled a laugh. "Now isn't this cozy?"

"All right," she muttered crossly, "you've made your point, Logan." She didn't dare open her eyes to look at him. She also knew better than to try to wriggle out of his grasp. She was in danger of losing her towel as it was, and it was questionable whether his was secure enough to defy the laws of gravity or not.

In an ardently pitched voice, he asked, "Have I, sweetheart?"

In Erin's estimation about a million goose bumps popped out on her flesh the moment his question reached her ears. She tried to tell herself he hadn't meant to sound so passionately sincere, but her brain had temporarily short-circuited. All she could concentrate on was the way her bottom fit so snugly against his thighs, and how warm and sleek his skin felt beneath the hands she had lifted to his chest. The combination of thick, corded muscles and crisp body hair made her hands itch to savor his shape and texture, and she was barely able to prevent herself from further exploration.

Goaded beyond endurance, she mumbled a petulant complaint. "I'm getting too hot, Logan."

Oh, goodness, she decided with fatalistic acceptance, she was an absolute genius when it came to devising stupid comments. In desperation she squinched her eyelids tighter together, and prayed that Logan would suddenly develop a hearing disorder. But in the next instant she realized his auditory facilities remained unimpaired, as his chest began to shake with suppressed laughter.

"That's only fair," he murmured when he was at last able to string together a coherent sentence, "since you raised my body temperature by quite a few degrees this morning."

In desperation, she insisted, "It was only a joke, for goodness' sake!"

"One that backfired, sweetness." As he spoke he lowered his head, and his mouth began to nuzzle her temple. "You know, for an Idaho farm girl you can be a sexy little baggage when you put your mind to it."

"Sexy?" she squeaked in protest. "I wasn't trying to be sexy. Well, not really."

"Whether you were or not isn't the point, Erin." His voice quietly persuasive, he added, "What really matters is that you turned me on. Now I want to know what you intend to do about it?"

"Don't you have a shut-off switch?" she questioned faintly.

Wickedly suggestive laughter greeted her inquiry. "Do you really want me to answer that?"

Her eyelids flew open, enabling her to glance at him. "Don't you dare!" she snapped in exasperation.

"Look, I've already apologized. Can't you be satisfied with that?"

As he shook his head his lips brushed against her ear, and the tip of his tongue began to trace its shape. "You're the one who decided to turn on the heat. Can't you think of a pleasanter way to satisfy me, angel?"

Erin inhaled sharply and began to push against his chest with flagging strength. But to her dismay her open hands lingered, defeating her purpose. The low groan of protest she uttered was rooted in despair. "Don't, Logan. I . . . this isn't funny anymore."

Logan redirected his mouth until it hovered just above her parted lips. She was right, he realized in shaken acceptance. Suddenly the situation he had created was no longer in the least amusing. The game had indefinably altered at some point, and the ache in his body was making him realize he'd been caught with a losing hand. God! He'd been insane to start something he wasn't prepared to finish.

He studied the face raised to his, and his heart struck a remorseful beat as he noticed its guarded vulnerability. "In case you haven't noticed, I've stopped laughing."

Drawing a shuddering breath, she whispered, "You . . . then you're not just making fun of me?"

"If I've been making fun of anyone it's myself," he grumbled hoarsely. "You tease me and I go a little crazy. Don't you realize you've practically got me on my knees, woman?"

Logan's admission was reenforced by his actions as he began to concentrate on kissing her, and Erin shivered in response. After first testing the resiliency of her mouth, his teeth gently scraped against the cord of her neck. As if that wasn't enough to drive her out of her mind, he opened his mouth wider until he could absorb the pulse that beat so violently against her throat.

Uttering a keening cry she arched her head back against his arm, the shoulder-length strands of her hair falling straight and free until they brushed his thigh. The tickling sensation caused a low moan to erupt from his chest, and he drew her closer. "Put your arms around me," he demanded with tender persuasion. "I need you to hold me, Erin."

Mindlessly she complied, her hands sliding over his shoulders until they were clutching the back of his head. His hair slipped between and around her fingers, as though the steam-dampened strands had a mind of their own. They contoured themselves to the shape of her hands, in much the same way her body was flowing into his, hard against soft, strong against weak, sleek against rounded. She could hear his heart pounding, or maybe it was her own. The confusion that was clouding her head seemed to be sapping rational thought, leaving pure sensation in its place.

"Logan, please," she groaned, without fully realizing what she was asking for.

"Yes," he gasped against her throat, replacing his lips with the palm of his hand. "I want to please you so badly I feel as if I'm coming apart."

There was a tiny smile on his mouth as it repeated its earlier journey, until it encountered the sweetness for which it searched. He teasingly traced the shape of her lips with the tip of his tongue, and drew back to admire his moistly glistening handiwork. Erin's lips were parted as though hungry for more, and Logan's eyes glowed with heated response. "You taste like wild honey, do you know that?"

There was wonder in the eyes that gazed back at him. "I do?"

As if to prove the truth of his assertion, Logan began kissing her fiercely, his lips slanting across hers in urgent demand. With a shaken moan she opened to him like a rosebud sipping rain, and his tongue surged inside to continue the ravishing exploration. It learned the texture and taste of her flesh. It sought submission and received a passionate flowering that stunned him. He felt her sharp little nails gouging his skin, and the kiss burned hotly out of control.

When she responded to this new depth of intimacy with a mewling cry of delight, his tongue plunged in a desperate attempt to capture the vibrations of her arousal. She clutched him more tightly, her entire being concentrating on the molten flow of heat spreading through her body. With shy hesitation her own tongue joined in the slick, fervent search for satisfaction, and this time it was Erin who caught his cry in her mouth.

Logan's body shuddered with convulsive force, but a last, lingering thread of sanity helped him regain a measure of control. With a muffled groan of protest he lifted his head, and felt himself aching from the top of his head to the soles of his feet. Abandoning her mouth was one of the hardest things he'd ever had to do, but this situation was becoming explosive. He wanted to lay her down and cover her sweet body with his. He wanted to watch her thighs part and open to him. He wanted to feel her heated depths surrounding him. Sweet Lord, he wanted to drive into her until there was no beginning or end for either of them!

But Erin deserved a tender wooing, he told himself, not caveman urgency on a hard wooden bench. She deserved candlelight and romantic music, champagne and flowers. She deserved cool, crisp sheets on a soft bed, and loving whispers in the darkness. She definitely deserved more than he was giving her, especially time to come to terms with her own sensuality. He was the one who'd started this, he thought grimly, and it was up to him to finish it while he was still able to pull back.

Logan tried to regulate his breathing, but the air was pumping from his lungs at an alarming rate. Pulling Erin tighter into his embrace, he buried his face against the sweetly scented hair on the crown of her head. "I picked a hell of a place to make love to you," he muttered with a strangled gasp. "We're going to smother to death if we don't get out of here, babe."

Erin sighed and ran a languid hand over his shoulder, admiring the tightness of sinew and moist flesh. "I'd die happy."

She wasn't doing his heart rate much good, but he was too elated by her innocent confession to care. With a triumphant grin he tossed back his head to try and restore order to the hair which had fallen over his forehead, and rose from the bench with her in his arms. "You would, huh?"

Meeting his gaze, Erin brushed back the recalcitrant strands with her fingertips. "Don't you know how much you mean to me, Logan? Before you came along I felt like an ugly duckling, but your touch has turned me into a swan. With your arms around me, I feel like the most beautiful woman alive."

"That's because you are," he whispered hoarsely, "but I don't want you to see me as some kind of plaster saint, Erin."

A small, secret smile curved her mouth. "I don't think you have to worry about that. You weren't exactly exhibiting saintlike qualities a few minutes ago."

"You know what I mean."

She chuckled at his affronted expression and tilted her head to one side. "Don't you want me to admire you?"

Logan lowered the radiator off switch with his shoulder and carried her out of the sauna. Squinting in the brighter light, he slowly began walking toward the frothing Jacuzzi. "Of course I do, but don't blind yourself to my faults. I'm just a man, with all the foibles and weaknesses inherent in the breed, Erin."

She peeked at him from beneath her lashes. "Are you going to continue convincing me, Mr. Sinclair?"

"You'd better believe it, Ms. Daniels."

Erin shivered, both at the tone of his voice and the steamy mist which was rising up from below to envelope them. Linking her hands together behind his neck, she shyly burrowed her face against his throat. "I've heard that making love in a hot tub is highly erotic."

"Oh, no you don't," he muttered grimly. "We'll give this a miss tonight."

She pressed a series of tiny kisses against his collarbone. "I'll go put on a suit if you're shy."

Logan choked on a laugh, but when she glanced up at him he glared at her. "I prefer the towel."

"It'll float off."

A grin slashed his face. "That's why I prefer the towel."

Placing a kiss against the corner of his mouth, she whispered, "I'm game if you are."

Logan's eyes held hers as he began to step into the Jacuzzi, but the sound of voices halted his descent. Erin's disappointment was evident in her voice when she murmured, "The cleaning crew."

"Thank God," Logan breathed fervently.

Seven

———

The soothing purr of the engine and the air-conditioned comfort of Logan's car proved to have an irresistible sedative effect on Erin's tired body, and she slept during the hour and a half drive into Sacramento. She looked endearingly young to the man who sent frequent glances in her direction, her somnolent body curled into the bucket seat beside him appearing no larger than a child's.

But she was all woman, and not for the first time Logan found himself wishing this weren't a working weekend for them. He hated the thought of sharing Erin with other people, especially after last night. His hands tensed on the wheel as he recalled their interlude in the sauna, and a muscle pulsed against his jaw as his teeth ground together. He had come perilously close to the edge with her, and he didn't know how long he was going to be able to continue holding out.

Erin gave of herself to others, to her work, and she made no secret of the fact that she wanted to give herself to him. She was willing to trust him, but the problem was he couldn't trust himself. The more he learned about her, the more terrified he became of hurting her. She was a forever kind of woman, and he was a temporary kind of man. The two just didn't mix, and that single, inescapable uncertainty was playing hell with his determination to do the right thing by her.

If he followed the urgings of his conscience he would end their personal relationship, but guilt had no power over the force of his desire for Erin. He wanted her more than he wanted air to breathe or food to eat, and he died a little inside at the thought of losing her. One day she would walk away from him, because he wasn't capable of giving her the commitment she would need for lasting happiness. But not yet, he thought painfully, not until he had impressed her sweetness on his soul. Although he cursed his own selfishness, he knew he wasn't strong enough to protect her from himself.

"Hello."

Logan's head turned at the huskily voiced greeting, tenderness filling him as he looked at her sleep-flushed face. "Good morning," he greeted softly. "I was beginning to wonder if you were ever going to wake up."

Erin stretched languidly and straightened to glance out of the window. "Where are we?"

"We're passing through Citrus Heights," he responded. "We'll be at our turnoff in about five minutes."

Her mouth flew open in surprise. "Do you mean I've slept the entire trip away?" she gasped incredulously. "You should have wakened me, Logan."

"I thought you should rest." He smiled at her guilty reaction. "You didn't get much sleep last night."

"And you did?" she questioned with mocking concern. "You had to drive all the way back home after dropping me off last night, so you got to bed later than I did."

"I didn't get to bed at all."

"Why not?"

Logan's grin widened at her scandalized expression. "I had too much on my mind."

"Don't you ever stop working?" she exclaimed disapprovingly.

Tongue-in-cheek, he drawled, "I wasn't working."

Twin flags of color darkened her cheeks while jealousy did the same to her thoughts. Instantly an image of Lorna Phelps rose in her mind, and she stiffened defensively. Late yesterday afternoon Logan's mother had called him at work, as Lorna had been quick to inform Erin. Logan had already left for his meeting, and Lorna's expression had been maliciously triumphant as she mentioned her intention of stopping by his place to deliver the message. "Logan has a lovely home, doesn't he?" she had added with sly calculation.

"I wouldn't know," Erin replied stiltedly. "I've never been there."

Erin had felt humiliated by the pitying sneer on Lorna's face. "How remiss of him, darling, but then that doesn't surprise me in the least. Logan only encourages visits from close friends and family. He prefers to do his . . . entertaining . . . elsewhere. Much less messy when he ends an affair.''

The memory of that taunting voice ate at Erin like a cancer, and her eyes flashed angrily as she looked at Logan. ''Was she waiting for you when you got home?''

''My housekeeper?'' Logan enquired innocently.

Erin clamped her teeth together, eventually spitting out a name in a voice filled with loathing. ''Lorna!''

''Are you jealous?''

She wanted to slap the pleased smirk off of his mouth, but instead sniffed disdainfully. ''Of course not, you raving egotist. I don't have any claim on you.''

''You do, you know.''

His gentle assertion only increased her fury, and she glowered even more fiercely. ''I do what?''

''Have a claim on me,'' he whispered.

Erin caught her breath, her mouth trembling with emotion. ''If I did you wouldn't have gone from me to . . .''

'' . . . to you,'' he concluded firmly.

Confused, she repeated, ''To me?''

''I spent the evening sprawled in a chair while I thought about you.''

''Oh,'' she remarked with a chagrined smile.

''Yes, oh,'' he laughed. ''Unfortunately, thinking of you didn't prove to be a relaxing pastime.''

In spite of his complaint, Erin looked very well satisfied with herself. ''You would have been better off in bed.''

"Perchance to dream?" he questioned with a negative shake of his head. "Erotic fantasies would have left me in worse shape than insomnia, honey."

Recalling the distinctly sensual flavor of her own dreams, Erin's cheeks took on the hue of a dusky rose. "Isn't that our turnoff ahead?" she questioned with mock brightness.

Logan's lips quirked with amusement as he gave his signal to depart the freeway, but he decided to change the subject and spare her blushes. With the confidence of a man who knows he will receive an affirmative answer, he asked, "Ready for your lecture tonight?"

For the rest of the journey they discussed the few changes they had decided to make in their conference schedule, and the next half hour was spent at the hotel's registration desk. Leaving Logan to check out the conference center, Erin followed a porter to her room. She tipped the man and glanced around without interest, not at all surprised by her cramped quarters.

Since Carrie had been on vacation the past couple of weeks it had been left to Lorna to make their reservations, and she lost no opportunity in making things as difficult for Erin as possible. But when they registered Logan hadn't been pleased to realize that their rooms were on different floors, she remembered, and if the charming Ms. Phelps wasn't careful he was soon going to smell a rat.

After a briskly refreshing shower, Erin felt human enough to rejoin Logan for the brunch that would officially open the conference. She checked her appearance before leaving the room, satisfied with her businesslike look in the oyster-white pantsuit she'd chosen to wear. The creamy material showed her light tan to advantage, and the tailored blue blouse with its wide collar and ruffled center pleat exactly matched the color of her eyes.

Departing the elevator at the main lobby, Erin was soon caught up in a flurry of activity. She was only scheduled to give a short welcoming speech during this initial meeting, but both she and Logan spent the next hour deluged with last-minute problems. The people in charge of registration hadn't arrived yet, the plane carrying his Los Angeles staff delayed by fog. When a flustered young bellboy dropped the box containing alphabetized name tags, the general air of confusion predictably increased.

With unflappable calm Erin seated herself at the bare registration table to sort out the latter problem, leaving a grumbling Logan to handle the more major difficulties. With half of her attention centered on her task and the other half on Logan, she worked at a slower pace than usual. Her admiring gaze followed him as he moved through the crowded lobby, the Italian cut of his charcoal-gray suit adding to his air of distinction. He smiled often and with infectious charm, and she noticed more than one woman following his tall figure with bemused eyes.

One in particular caught Erin's attention, and her mouth tightened in annoyance. The tall, statuesque redhead had plastered herself to Logan's side like a limpet and Erin didn't miss the avaricious possessiveness in her expression when she looked up at her boss. She also didn't miss the air of intimacy that accompanied their greeting to each other, especially when the other woman reached up and pulled Logan's head down for a brief but telling kiss. It seemed that model 'he'd once dated hadn't been the only redhead to find favor with him, she decided petulantly.

"Monica and Logan make a striking couple, don't they?"

Erin's head swiveled to meet a pair of amused brown eyes, set in a boyishly handsome face, which were correctly assessing her disgruntled mood. "Is that her name?"

Hitching up his slacks, her informant seated himself on the edge of the table. "Mmm, and mine's Tom Masters. I'm manager of the Sacramento club and a member of Logan's board of directors. I'm sorry I wasn't able to make it to the party he threw for you." He grinned and shrugged his shoulders a bit self-consciously. "I was curious to meet this Erin Daniels the grapevine's been buzzing about, but I was attending my own engagement bash that evening."

"Congratulations," she responded with a smile. "Is your finacée here with you?"

"She'll be meeting me for a drink after the banquet this evening." The twinkle in his eyes deepened as he added, "I tried to talk her into an early honeymoon night, but she's an old-fashioned girl thanks to my future father-in-law. The old man wouldn't just chase me with a shotgun, he'd shoot me with it."

Although Erin laughed, the sound held a distracted note. Unwillingly her eyes had once again wandered in Logan's direction, and she didn't like his absorption with the lovely Monica. "I hope I have an opportunity to meet your fiancée, Tom."

"You don't have to worry, you know." As she slanted a startled glance at him, he said, "Although

Monica never says die, that affair's been over with for a long time. She became a little too possessive for Logan's taste."

Erin's shrug was too stiff to portray the carelessness she wished. "I don't know what you mean."

Tom grimaced self-consciously, his gaze apologetic. "Blame my unruly tongue on being in love," he said quietly. "One tends to recognize the condition in others."

Erin decided to let the comment pass, instead focusing her complete attention on Logan's companion. "She's very beautiful."

Her voice held a wistfulness the other man was quick to note and even quicker to refute. "Beauty without the character to back it up palls after a while, especially with a man like Logan. He's not the playboy the press makes him out to be, Erin."

She glanced up at him curiously. "You sound like you know him rather well."

"We were in the army together, and when we were discharged I went to work for him. That was nearly ten years ago now, but with me based in Sacramento we don't see as much of each other as we used to." His mouth formed a teasing grin as he leaned forward, his voice a confiding whisper. "Maybe that's all to the good since I'm about to become a staid married man. If Nora ever found out about some of the wild and woolier stunts Logan and I pulled in our misspent youth, she'd more than likely shove her engagement ring down my throat."

"Aren't you afraid I'll spill the beans?"

"Not a bit of it," he replied cheerfully. "You look much too softhearted to kick a man when he's down. My fragile ego is safe with you."

A terse voice sounded from beside them. "Your ego is about as fragile as a cement block, buddy."

Erin felt flustered as she met Logan's enigmatic gaze, embarrassed at having been caught discussing him with his friend. Averting her eyes toward the other man, she watched as he jumped to his feet and extended his hand. "Hey, it's good to see you again, Logan."

Erin thought Logan's smile seemed a trifle forced, but the warmth of his greeting convinced her she was imagining things. "It's good to see you too, Tom. How's life been treating you?"

"I can't complain," Tom drawled with a significant glance at Erin. "I'm in love."

When a pair of brooding green eyes narrowed on her reddening cheeks, Erin rushed into inarticulate speech. "Don't you . . . I mean, do you think I should wait to hand out these name tags until after we've eaten, Logan?"

He nodded abruptly, his expression distant as he glanced down at the watch strapped to his wrist. "That's what I came over to suggest. We're already a half hour behind schedule, and the hotel management will be getting antsy if we delay our brunch any longer. We can finish the registration proceedings later."

The hours that followed were tiring but productive, and by the time dinner was over there was a suppressed air of excitement in the banquet room. As Logan had known they would, his employees were charmed by Erin's air of shy enthusiasm and impressed with her intelligence. As had happened during the previous two conferences, she infected everyone with her belief in and enthusiasm for the new project. Her afternoon classes had been very well received, and after hearing some of the comments regarding her Logan had been near to bursting with pride.

Yet along with pride came a niggling sense of unease, and as she rose from the chair beside him he attempted to come to terms with his conflicting emotions. His eyes ran caressingly over her upright figure as she crossed the stage and stepped up to the podium. The vivid red gown she wore screamed elegance, the smallness of her waist emphasized by a silver medallion belt. Matching earrings swung from the lobes of her delicate ears, and a similarly designed brooch was centered between the draped bodice which lovingly molded the rounded fullness of her breasts.

Logan had taken one look at her tonight and felt his hackles rising, a circumstance which was happening too frequently for his peace of mind. This morning he'd even had the urge to slug one of his best and oldest friends, and Tom had only been talking to Erin. He was disgusted by his jealousy, and for the first time in his life he was uncertain of his own motives.

It was like being divided in half, he decided cynically. One part of him was pleased with the positive changes in Erin's appearance and personality, while another, more self-centered area of his mind felt threatened by her emerging self-confidence. She no longer needed to remain at his side during functions such as this, clinging to him as if he was a familiar port in a stormy sea. Instead she laughed and sparkled like a multifaceted jewel, and drew others to her with effortless ease.

Of course his uncertainty over his relationship with Erin was his own fault. He was the one holding her at arm's length, and if he was climbing the walls as a result he had nobody to blame but himself. She certainly was open enough about her feelings toward him. Every look she gave him, every touch, no matter how casual it seemed, was pure provocation. She wanted more than the avuncular attention he was paying her, and she was no longer too shy to let him know it!

The sound of clapping broke Logan from his reverie. As Erin returned to her place beside him he gave her a strained smile of approval, and walked to the podium to address the audience. He bent toward the microphone, which Erin had lowered to suit her own height. "This concludes the working part of our conference, ladies and gentlemen. Later in the year Ms. Daniels and I will be visiting each of your establishments individually to help you implement the procedures we've outlined today. But right now I suggest we leave the banquet hall to be cleared, and retire to the adjacent lounge where a band has been provided for your entertainment. Erin and I hope you enjoy the rest of your evening as much as we have enjoyed your involvement in this conference. So now... let's party, people!"

A firm knock on her door roused Erin from the light doze she'd fallen into upon returning to her hotel room. With a murmur of dismay she jumped up from the bed, grabbing her gold chenille robe from the closet as she hurried across the carpeted floor. Slipping her arms through the batwing sleeves, she grimaced at her rumpled reflection in the mirrored closet doors.

After leaving the party she hadn't bothered to undress completely, at the time too exhausted to do more than remove the barest necessities. She had collapsed on top of the bedspread in just a thin slip and panties, sighing with pleasure as the air conditioner bathed her heated flesh with coolness. She had danced until she felt as though her feet would fall off, but she couldn't honestly say she'd enjoyed herself. Logan's inexplicable surliness all evening had but paid to that.

That dratted man was driving her crazy, she thought with a scowl. He had spent the latter part of the evening surrounded by an entourage of admiring females, with one redhead quite disgustingly obvious in her attentions. Yet every time their gazes locked across the crowded dance floor, he had had the nerve to glare at her! Well, at least she hadn't let him think she was bothered by his miniature harem. She had laughed and flirted and thoroughly enjoyed herself. "In a pig's eye," she decided morosely as she opened the door.

Lifting a self-conscious hand to smooth some kind of order into her tangled hair, she greeted the unsmiling man in front of her with curt politeness. "I'm sorry I didn't have a chance to tell you good night, but I was too tired to fight my way through the crowd."

"I told you I wanted to talk to you before you went to bed."

She angled her chin with unvoiced belligerence. "Then I must apologize for forgetting," she stated abruptly. "I was exhausted, and decided to leave the party early. I didn't think you'd object, but I suppose I should have asked your permission to withdraw. After all, socializing has become a big part of my job, hasn't it?''

"Too much so,'' he ground out harshly, "and you know damn well I wouldn't have minded you leaving early. You've been run off your feet all day."

Logan stared at her flushed cheeks and rosebud mouth, now slightly parted in a revealing yawn. Stiffly he muttered, "May I come in for a minute?"

He seemed unusually tense, and with a puzzled glance at his unrevealing features Erin stepped back and motioned him into the room. As he strode forward, his eyes quickly scanned his surroundings with a critical gaze. "This room is smaller than I'd realized," he remarked with an edge to his voice. "My own accomodations are three times this size."

"But then you're the boss," she responded lightly. "This one is perfectly adequate for my needs, Logan."

"That may be, but I instructed Lorna to reserve two suites on the same floor. We are not only on different floors, but this rabbit hutch can hardly be termed a suite."

Erin subdued a grin as she remembered her own first impression upon arrival, and realized that Logan was reacting exactly as she'd thought he would. Although tastefully decorated in soothing blue-and-green accents, with floral floor-length drapes matching the bedspread, the room was cramped and overfurnished. Her bed stood on a raised dais to separate it from the living area, which held a television on a swivel stand, a short blue couch and matching easy chair, a small table in front of the window with two straight-backed chairs, and a minuscule wet bar in one corner. The green-and-cream tiled bathroom wasn't much larger than the closet, she remembered with another surge of amusement.

During the two previous trips they'd taken together Logan had never done more than wish her good night at her door, so he didn't realize that this room was quite the nicest Lorna had *ever* seen fit to reserve for her. If he wanted to see a real cracker box, he should have visited her rooms in Eureka or Santa Rosa. She could have complained, but she was certain that would have been playing into Lorna Phelps's hands. Considering her already strained relationship with the Dragon Lady, Erin strove to be conciliatory. She certainly didn't want to give the other woman an opportunity to accuse her of trying to gain Logan's favor by tattling about her behind her back.

Without batting an eye at the lie, Erin said, "Lorna must have misunderstood your instructions."

Logan's eyes narrowed in an assessing stare, as he remarked cynically, "I think you know better than that."

Erin shrugged and smiled at him. "I'm not exactly her favorite person, but don't let it bother you. I'm not terribly fond of her myself."

To her surprise he scowled at her levity. "That's no reason for her to slight you at every opportunity, Erin, or did you imagine me blind and deaf to the little games she's been playing?"

"It really doesn't matter, Logan." Her voice held a soothing note as she informed him, "No one pays any attention to her."

He ignored her pleading expression, his body rigid with disapproval as he paced the room. Lowering himself onto the couch, he leaned back with a muttered curse. "It matters when I hear the gossip she's been spreading about us, but I'm too damn tired right now to talk about Lorna. Thank heavens we decided we could get by with a one-day conference this time. I'm a bit frayed about the edges."

He didn't look in the least ragged, Erin decided admiringly. With his tuxedo jacket discarded and his dress shirt partially unbuttoned he appeared rakishly attractive, especially when he brushed his rumpled hair from his forehead with an impatient hand. But he did seem unusually tired, and she joined him on the couch with a concerned frown. "You need to slow down a little, Logan."

A muscle pulsed in his jaw as he looked at her. "Let's not get on the subject of my needs, Erin. This isn't the time or the place, and I'm not in a forgiving-enough frame of mind to let you off lightly."

She straightened her spine and glared at him. "Just what should I be forgiven for?"

"I think you know," he retorted fiercely, the hands resting on his knees clenching into fists. "I didn't find your behavior this evening to my taste."

"Oh, didn't you?" she questioned angrily. "Let me tell you, yours wasn't exactly exemplary."

His mouth compressed into a tight line. "I don't know what you mean."

"I mean your ex-lover," she snapped. "The way she was hanging all over you made me sick."

"My relationship with Monica was over long be-fore we met, and at least I didn't leave the lounge with her."

"You certainly didn't act as if your relationship was a thing of the past."

"Don't try and shift the focus of this conversation onto me, because I have a few doubts of my own, Erin. What was the idea of going off with Masters?"

Erin's brow crinkled in confusion. "Tom Masters? I didn't go anywhere with him."

"I'm in a position to know that the blond boy wonder of Citrus Heights is a fast mover with the la-dies," he sneered, "and I saw the two of you leaving together with my own eyes."

Erin gasped with sudden awareness. "You're jeal-ous!"

In a single, sinuous movement he leaned forward and grasped her by the shoulders, administering a slight shake as he did so. "Too right I'm jealous," he muttered. "I damn near followed the two of you! In-stead I phoned your room and got no answer. Were you so bowled over by his charm that you let him talk you into visiting his, Erin? Were you?"

Each question was punctuated with another shake, each one firmer than the one before. But Erin didn't mind this display of masculine aggression in the slightest. She was too delighted by his possessiveness to be angry. "We walked out of the lounge and reached the lobby, where his fiancée was waiting for him. The three of us had a quiet drink in the bar, and then I came up here alone. I was too tired to return to the party."

Logan's fingers slid over her robe, his eyes apologetic as he rested his hands on her shoulders. "I'm sorry, but you've changed so much these past few weeks. You've got me spinning in circles."

"I've been a bit dizzy myself," she admitted wryly.

"You're so beautiful I'm tempted to slug every man who looks at you, and you've come out of your shell with a vengeance. Sometimes I wonder where my shy, retiring little mouse has gone."

"Oh, Logan," she whispered in dismay. "I thought you were proud of my new sophistication. You're always complimenting me on my appearance, and telling me what a good impression I've made on your friends and business associates."

Logan withdrew his hands from her with a sigh, and leaned forward with his elbows resting against his splayed knees. Linking his fingers together, he stared down at the blue-and-green flecked carpet with an absentminded expression. "I am and you have," he muttered disparagingly. "You've been doing a terrific job for me, and if all I was concerned with was the program there would be no problem. It's my own lack of efficiency I'm having difficulty with."

Erin scooted closer to him and laid her head on his bicep. "Why is that?" she questioned softly.

He glanced down at her upturned face, his mouth quirking sardonically. "You know damn well I'm frustrated to the point of insanity, Ms. Daniels."

"And you also know the solution, Mr. Sinclair."

Logan inhaled sharply, his senses aroused by her calmly voiced statement. "Are you trying to seduce me again?" he murmured huskily.

Erin laughed and rubbed her cheek against his arm. "I'm waiting for you to seduce me, but you're not making a very good job of it."

With an exasperated moan he pressed her against the cushioned back of the couch, his mouth finding her own with unerring accuracy. Erin's lips parted to welcome the evocative thrust of his tongue, her own cry muffled by the force of his kiss. Her hands slipped over his arms, finally coming to rest at the base of his skull. Her fingers disappeared within the thick, soft strands of his hair, and she shuddered as his palm cradled the pointed fullness of her breast.

"Logan," she groaned as he gently squeezed her burgeoning flesh. "You make me burn when you touch me."

In frenzied enjoyment her lips sought out every inch of his face she could reach, finally coming to rest against the hollow of his throat. She squirmed beneath his weight, twisting her hips until she felt his hard male outline throbbing hotly against the flowering portals of her womanhood. Now her robe was open, revealing the silhouette of her breasts beneath her slip. He gasped and uttered a strangled growl, his mouth enveloping her nipple through the flimsy material.

Logan began to suckle with languid pleasure, clasping her buttocks as he rocked slowly against her in unmistakable rhythm. Pressure built and pooled inside of her stomach in a liquid blaze like nothing she'd ever experienced, and Erin began to tug his shirt from his pants with urgent insistence. Slipping her hands beneath the loosened folds, she sighed with satisfaction and began to trace his hair-roughened chest with trembling fingers.

A shudder shook him, and his muscles tensed as he withdrew. "Erin, are you protected?" he questioned tersely.

For a moment she stared at him blankly, and then her features crumpled in distress. Closing his eyes, he straightened with difficulty. "That's what I thought."

"I'm sorry," she whimpered, shaking with unfulfilled desire. "I'm so sorry, Logan."

Tenderly he brushed back her hair, his eyes warm with understanding as he gazed at her. "So am I, but the responsibility for birth control should be shared. Anyway, neither of us could have anticipated this happening tonight."

"Some modern woman of the world I am," she muttered in disgust. "I should have made an appointment with my doctor weeks ago."

Logan laughed ruefully and tapped her on the end of her tip-tilted nose. "Will you call me a chauvinistic pig if I admit that I'm pleased you haven't learned the basic rudiments of starting an affair?"

"Oh, I don't know," she teased. "I thought I was doing a good job with the basics a few minutes ago."

She ran a lazy forefinger from a bare bicep to the crook of his elbow, smiling her satisfaction when he shivered in response. With a groan he lifted her hand, taking the tormenting little digit into the sensuous warmth of his mouth. Erin gasped at the evocative caress, her eyes still dark with arousal. "The sign in the window of the drugstore downstairs says they're open twenty-four hours," she reminded him in a voice so faint as to be almost indistinguishable. "Why don't you pay them a quick visit and put us both out of our misery?''

"Because I've had time to come to my senses."

"You are the most stubborn, dictatorial, irritating..."

A devilish light appeared in his eyes a split second before he bit her finger. Jerking her hand back with a startled yelp, she scowled at him. "You sure know how to destroy a romantic mood, Sinclair."

With a resonant chuckle Logan got to his feet and pulled her up beside him. "I've had quite a lot of practice fending off a certain amorous female this past month."

"And practice has made you perfect," she groused as she accompanied him to the door. "What I'm wondering is when you're going to realize there's no longer any need for you to protect me from myself."

He gave her a darkly brooding look and hurriedly thrust open the door. "You're getting there, baby!"

Erin watched him walk away from her, a tiny grin curling the edges of her mouth. Yes, she was getting there, she thought complacently. No longer plagued by uncertainties, she had become a woman who knew exactly what she wanted. His name was Logan Sinclair, and he colored her world.

Eight

Erin uttered a dismayed exclamation as she heard Logan's car pull up outside. They were leaving for Monterey this morning, and when he'd told her how early he intended to pick her up she hadn't uttered a single protest. Which had been a foolish omission, since she wasn't what one would call a morning person. In fact it took at least two cups of coffee before she could be considered human. Throwing a frantic glance around the chaotic mess that used to pass for her room, she felt the urge to tear her hair out by the roots. If she had more of it she probably would!

From the time her alarm sounded, she'd been in a frenzy of indecision. Nothing suited her disgruntled mood. Not her favorite gold-and-rust pantsuit, nor her new emerald-green blouse and cream-colored skirt. Out of desperation she'd settled on a comfortable pair of stonewashed jeans and a ruffly, blue-and-white spaghetti-strapped sun top that left most of her shoulders bare. She wasn't particularly satisfied by her choice, but she had a feeling Logan would be.

The outer door was locked at night and as she heard the buzzer sound she flinched in consternation. Before long the whole house was going to be awake, and at six o'clock on a Saturday morning no one would be smiling as they went on their way. Running to the window, she fumbled with the rusty latch and shoved it up far enough to get her head through the opening. "Logan," she hissed as loudly as she dared, "I'll be right down."

Logan backed off the porch and grinned up at her. "Don't tell me my efficient Ms. Daniels is running late again?"

"Don't be sarcastic." She stuck her tongue out at him, chuckling when he gave her an exaggerated look of offense. "Your efficient Ms. Daniels couldn't make up her mind what to wear."

His eyebrows peaked roguishly. "Need any help? I'm pretty handy with buttons and snaps."

"I just bet you are!"

Logan eyed the flush pinkening her cheeks, and uttered a full-throated laugh. "Whatever are you imagining, Ms. Daniels?"

"Oh, hush," she whispered impatiently. "Teasing a person this early in the day is obscene."

Propelling herself backward, she tried to close the window only to have it catch halfway down. Uttering an impolite word that alluded to all ancient houses with wooden frames that swelled, this one in particular, she pushed so hard she nearly cracked the glass when it finally came unstuck. She winced at the thunderous bang that resulted, but didn't pause to think of a new descriptive word.

Hurrying across the floor, she grabbed a brush from the top of her scarred and stained walnut dresser, and began to run it impatiently through her hair. She had planned to put it up, but there was no time for that now. Grimacing as the stiff bristles scraped against her scalp, she decided that this was turning out to be one terrific morning. She didn't pause to check her reflection in the mirror as she threw down her brush and bent to pick up her luggage. The way she was feeling, she could look like the most beautiful woman in the world and still not be satisfied.

Her suitcase bumped against one leg and her briefcase against the other as she struggled down the stairs, but she didn't let the thought of a few bruises bother her. She couldn't wait to get to Monterey. She'd been looking forward to this trip all week, and she was determined not to allow anything to spoil her pleasure . . . especially her own grouchiness.

Determined not to let her disgruntled mood put a damper on their drive up the coast, she planted a brilliant smile on her face for Logan's benefit. "I'm ready to go."

The grumpiness hidden beneath Erin's smile wasn't lost on her employer. He had long since realized her aversion to mornings, and his lips quivered with amusement as she trudged purposely toward him. "So I see. Let me carry those for you."

Stepping off the porch with more alacrity than grace, Erin handed him her cases. She found herself staring at Logan with the blatant intensity of a starving feline. He was putting her belongings in the trunk of his car, and as he bent forward the muscles in his back and arms rippled and his trim buttocks tightened. Immediately the saliva in Erin's mouth dried up, and she wished she still had her suitcase to sit on. Muttering dire imprecations beneath her breath, she practically tore the handle off the car door in her hurry to get inside.

When Logan slid behind the wheel, Erin couldn't make herself look at him. A change had occurred in their relationship this past week, an unspoken awareness of what differences this weekend might bring to their relationship. But since Logan hadn't actually stated his intentions to make love to her, she didn't quite know how to act around him. Should she make a witty remark alluding to her own expectations?

No, that wouldn't do, since she doubted if she was sophisticated enough to pull it off without blushing like a schoolgirl. Nibbling the inside of her cheek, she stared through the windshield as if mesmerized by the passing scenery. But in actuality her eyes were blind to the traffic and her surroundings. The silence stretching between her and Logan was becoming oppressive, and she felt nervous enough to jump straight through the open sunroof.

Logan, too, was uneasy. His hands held the steering wheel in a death grip, and he kept slanting troubled glances in Erin's direction. She'd been nervous and ill at ease around him for days, and he wondered what the hell had gone wrong. Everything had been fine until . . . until that interlude in her hotel room last weekend. Could Erin be as frustrated as he was? Logan was amazed at how much a single thought could bolster his spirits.

Still preoccupied, he drew his bottom lip between his teeth and his right front tire promptly collided with a pothole. "Damn!"

Erin's head swiveled in his direction, her expression startled. "What's wrong?"

Expelling his breath in a disgusted whoosh, he muttered sheepishly, "I bit my lip."

Erin choked on a gasp, which accelerated into a delighted chuckle. She shook her head in mock reproval, but her blue eyes were brimming with suppressed hilarity as she asked, "What did you want to do that for?"

Pain was a small price to pay for the return of laughter in a pair of lovely blue eyes, and Logan was determined to keep it that way. Fastening his gaze on her smiling mouth with lazy deliberation, he murmured huskily, "Just practicing, sweetheart."

Although momentarily agitated by his teasing comment, Erin was relieved to be back on familiar footing with Logan. The miles passed between them, and by the time they stopped at a small roadside diner for breakfast her spirits were light and she was ravenously hungry.

They reached the outskirts of Monterey shortly before nine o'clock. It was already warm, the sun's rays dispersing the thin, misty fog shrouding the coastline. "It's going to be a scorcher today," Erin remarked, rolling down her window so she could enjoy the salt-scented ocean breeze.

"The weather forecast predicts record highs for this weekend," Logan informed her. "It's a pity we'll be spending it working."

Erin's heart sank at his words, but she sent him an encouraging smile. "We do have an awful lot to get through if we hope to remain on schedule, Logan. There will be other visits to Monterey."

Her attempt to soothe his irritation failed, and Logan pulled into the health club's parking lot with a rueful grimace. "From now on in we're going to be running flat out, and for the first time in my adult life I find myself resenting my work." Shutting off the engine, he speared her with a mocking glance. "You've never complained about the hectic pace I've set, and it isn't good for you to suppress your emotions, Erin. So go ahead and tell me I'm a workaholic. I promise not to fire you."

"You're a workaholic," she stated obligingly.

He groaned in disgust, and shook his head. "What's worse, I'm turning you into one."

"I don't mind."

Logan leaned his arm against the back of her bucket seat, and leaned toward her. Her breath caught in her throat as he tenderly brushed his mouth against her own. "I do," he whispered. "I'd like to have you all to myself for a change."

"I . . . I'd like that, too, Logan."

"Would you?"

Unable to withstand the ardor burning in his unblinking gaze, she averted her eyes and nodded an affirmative. Tracing the rounded softness of her cheek with the back of his hand, his knuckles drifted down her jawline to the tip of her chin. Slowly he tilted her head back with gentle pressure, and her wistful expression caused his heart to skip a beat. "We won't be working nonstop," he informed her gruffly. "Somehow we'll manage to snatch a few hours on the beach before we leave. Have you ever body-surfed?"

"The one time I tried a wave knocked me down and I swallowed half the ocean." She wrinkled her nose and grinned. "It wasn't the most comfortable experience of my life. My stomach objected quite violently to an influx of salt water."

Although he tried to appear solemn, there was a twinkle in his eyes as he said, "Will you let me teach you if I promise not to let you drown?"

Her response was unaffectedly eager. "I'd love it!"

Erin stared down at the papers covering the desk that had been provided for her, and her lashes lowered to ease the burning in her aching and scratchy eyes. Remembering those tentative plans she and Logan had made upon their arrival seemed hilariously optimistic now, only she wasn't laughing. Considering the work that still needed to be done, she was certain that Logan's beach house was the closest they were going to get to the ocean.

From the moment they had entered this complex they hadn't had a moment to call their own. Most of their time had been tied up in meetings with the club's senior staff members, which had carried over through a hastily eaten lunch at a nearby restaurant. Dinner had also been a working meal, and by the end of the day she'd been exhausted.

Erin had fallen asleep in the car when Logan drove further up the coast to his beach house, which he'd earlier told her he'd bought while his club was being completed. "I love being within sight and sound of the sea," he had said. "Eventually I'd like to move my base of operations to Monterey and live here permanently."

Although the drive wasn't a long one, her sleep had been so deep she'd been disoriented and confused when they arrived at their destination. She'd only gotten the briefest impression of a sprawling, weathered wooden structure inlaid with a great deal of glass, before Logan ushered her through the front door. The bedroom he led her to was decorated in warm peach tones, but the only thing that had really interested her at that moment was the comfortable-looking double bed. She had showered and brushed her teeth in the en-suite bathroom, and had been dead to the world within twenty minutes.

Rotating the pads of her fingers against her throbbing temples, Erin's mouth twisted into a humorless smile. This morning certainly hadn't given her much opportunity to inspect Logan's oceanfront home. She'd forgotten to set her travel alarm, and awakened to the unfamiliar cry of gulls outside her bedroom window. She had groped on the nightstand for her wristwatch, and when she noticed the lateness of the hour she'd landed on the carpet with a thud that had vibrated from the soles of her feet to the top of her head.

A brief shower had cleared some of the sleep from her gritty eyes, but it hadn't done much to restore her composure. She was one of those people who, no matter how much they planned ahead, were fated to lateness. When she'd previously traveled with Logan, he'd only been amused by the abject apologies she'd given him when the inevitable occurred. But she had vowed that this trip would be different, she recalled with a disdainful sniff. She'd planned to impress him with her timely efficiency, instead of running around like a flustered chicken.

A tiny dimple popped out beside Erin's mouth when she remembered storming out of her room, only to run full tilt into Logan. He had given a grunt of protest as he reached out to steady her, but there had been amusement in his voice as he asked, "Where are you off to in such a hurry?"

With contrition darkening her eyes, she'd gasped, "I'm sorry I'm late. I was so tired last night I forgot to set my alarm, and I'm only thankful the seagulls woke me. Otherwise I'd still be dead to the world."

He had silenced her in the most satisfactory way imaginable, she recalled dreamily. He'd drawn her into his arms, his mouth warm and heart-stoppingly sensual. By the time he freed her tingling lips she'd forgotten all about being late, her thoughts centered solely on him. "Damn noisy gulls," he complained huskily. "I was looking forward to dragging you out of bed myself."

Erin was still picturing the look in Logan's mesmerizing jade eyes when the office door flew open, and the object of her thoughts strode up to her desk like a general commanding an army. "Come on, Erin," he said cheerfully. "We're busting out of this joint."

She simply stared at him in surprise, and with a huge grin on his face he grabbed her hands and pulled her out of her chair. He had dragged her halfway

across the floor before she managed to splutter a protest. "But L-Logan, I'm not finished with..."

"Yes you are," he interrupted, slamming the office
door shut behind them and continuing down the hall.

"But I have to..."

"No you don't," he corrected with maddening
congeniality.

Erin was having trouble keeping up with his long-
legged strides, and she was panting by the time they
reached the central lobby. Not only that, but as they
passed by open doorways grinning faces seemed to be
popping out of the woodwork to mark their passage.
One man, she was rushed past too swiftly to recognize who, even had the temerity to call out, "Way to
go, boss!"

"I'm going to kill you for this," she muttered, her
face as red as a beet as Logan shoved her through the
front door. "I am going to tie you up and..."

He wrapped an arm around her waist and practically carried her to the car, an unmistakable gleam in
his eyes as he drawled, "Sounds kinky, but whatever
turns you on."

"I'll turn you on, you...!"

"I'm counting on it."

As he spoke, Logan trapped her between the side of
the car and his big, hard body. Her eyes widened with
a physical awareness so complete she went limp, only
the pressure of their taut frames preventing her from
slipping to the ground. Her breasts were in tingling
contact with his hard chest, and his hips were locked
against her quivering belly. "Logan," she moaned,
"I..."

Her voice trailed off into silence as his hands rose to cradle her face. For a long, breathtaking instant he looked at her, his eyes holding a question she was too shattered to respond to verbally. But her expression must have been more revealing than she realized, because with a low groan he bent his head and captured her mouth with hungry satisfaction. Since invading her office he'd only allowed her to complete one lousy sentence, but suddenly she didn't mind, at all. If there was one thing Logan was good at, she decided dreamily, it was shutting her up!

They had driven several miles before Erin collected her thoughts enough to ask, "Where are we going?"

"First home to change, and then I'm taking you to a restaurant on Cannery Row for dinner," he replied. "It's one of the original buildings from Steinbeck's day, an old converted warehouse within a few feet of the beach. They specialize in fresh seafood."

Erin began to tremble as she looked at him, suddenly knowing that the last thing she wanted was to share him with a lot of strangers. "Are you craving seafood?" she probed tentatively.

He flashed her a sidelong glance, his gaze heated enough to blister paint off a wall at forty paces. "Let's just say that it's the one craving I'm prepared to satisfy."

An odd roaring sounded in her ears, carrying the thud of her heartbeat with it. Moistening her lips, she said, "If you stop at the grocery store, I can cook our dinner tonight."

This time his glance held concern. "If you're too tired to go out, I'll pick up a pizza on the way home. Once you've eaten you can go right to bed."

"But I'd enjoy fixing us a meal," she protested. "You must be sick of eating out."

He weighed her words for a minute, and then suggested an alternative. "Why don't I pick up some steaks for the barbecue, so you won't be stuck with all the work?"

"That sounds wonderful," she replied eagerly. "Do you like corn on the cob?"

"What's a barbecue without it?"

With a pleased sigh she murmured, "Steak, steaming corn dripping with butter, warm wheat rolls, and fresh canteloupe for a starter. How about chocolate cake for dessert?"

"Are you going to bake it for me with your own two hands?"

"No, but I'll watch it defrost if you like."

Giving a growl of laughter, he turned into the grocery store parking lot with his tires squealing. "You certainly know how to tempt a man."

"Do I?" she asked with sparkling eyes. Then she grimaced, and gave a disgusted shake of her head. "Why is it that most of the foods we enjoy are nutritional disasters?"

He placed an admonishing finger over her lips, and gestured behind him with an outspread thumb. "You left the dietitian back there, so not another word out of you. Now move 'em up and head 'em out, woman, before I expire from starvation."

Saluting him smartly, she reached for the handle of the door. "Yes, sir, Mr. Sinclair. Your wish is my command."

"God, I hope so," he muttered beneath his breath as he exited the car.

* * *

Cool, wet sand left by the receding tide squished between Erin's toes as she stood on the shore beside Logan. They had taken a relaxing stroll along the beach after dinner, only retracing their steps when the heat of the day was replaced by a brisk ocean breeze. They arrived back at the beach house just in time to watch the sun disappear below the horizon, leaving behind crimson and silver streaks in the sky.

Erin shivered, but not from the wind seeping through her flimsy cotton blouse. Her trembling was an inner reaction to the man standing so tall by her side, his hand clasped tightly around her own. He was wearing nothing but a ragged pair of cutoffs, his feet as bare as her own. She glanced at him and thought he looked wonderful, but it was the way he made her feel that was wonderful. These past hours had held a dreamlike quality of shared laughter and companionable silences, as though she and Logan had escaped into a world of their own. She never wanted to wake up.

"I love this time of evening."

Erin's words drew Logan's gaze, and he nodded his understanding. "The twilight, where for a few magical moments night and day come together to form a perfect balance. Both an end and a beginning, a reflection of the past and a promise of the future."

Gently he turned her toward him, his hands coming to rest on her shoulders. "You remind me of the twilight, Erin."

Her breath became trapped in her lungs as she sought the truth in his eyes. "I do?"

One finger rose to trace her mouth, his touch as light as leaves blown on the wind. "You wipe away the lonely shadows of my past and give me hope for to-morrow.''

Quick tears flooded her eyes, and she lowered her lashes to prevent their flow. "I . . . feel the same way about you, Logan."

He drew her closer until their bodies were locked together in a fervent embrace, and he pressed his face against her soft, fragrant hair. "I want you so much," he whispered in broken accents. "I want to make love with you and to you and for you. I want to belong to you and have you belong to me. I want to wake up in the morning with you in my arms, and watch twilight give birth to the dawn while the scent of your body still lingers on my skin."

Erin's trembling increased until she was a quaking mass of emotion in his arms. With a muffled cry she buried her lips against his warm throat, and mur-mured, "I feel as though I've needed you forever, Logan. I want you, too."

With a joyous exclamation he bent down and lifted her against him, his kiss blending with their laughter as he whirled her around and around in dizzying cir-cles. Erin's hands cradled his neck, her mouth open and giving beneath his. Their heartbeats echoed the pounding of the surf, and their passion exploded into a hot, molten fire as Logan began to carry his pre-cious burden across the sand.

Nine

The enormity of the decision she'd just made struck
Erin when Logan's bedroom door closed behind them.
After tonight there would be no going back for either
of them. She was suddenly frightened...not of Logan...but of herself. She wanted desperately to give
him all that he asked of her, but was doubtful of her
ability to do so. With his looks and wealth he had always had his choice of lovers, beautiful and worldly
women who knew how to please a man. While she had
no practical experience to guide her, and even less sophistication. What if she proved to be a disappointment to him?

Logan felt the tremor that shook her, and saw the
anxiety darkening her eyes. With a reassuring murmur he paused in the middle of the room, his face

softening with tenderness as he looked down at her. "Do you want to change your mind, Erin?"

She shook her head with an alacrity that brought a smile to his lips, but the humor didn't reach his eyes as he studied her vulnerable features for long, tension-filled moments. Then he gently set her on her feet and quite deliberately distanced himself from her. As he reached the far side of the room, he lifted the latch on the white-painted French doors which gave access to a small balcony overlooking the sea.

Slowly she followed, and paused in the doorway to study him. He was bending forward, his long-fingered hands gripping the wrought-iron balcony rail, and moonlight enhanced the taut outline of his body. He looked so lonely, she thought with painful awareness, his silhouette that of a man who had drawn into himself with inexplicable suddenness. She could almost feel the distress emanating from him, and she shivered with dread as she moved toward him. "What's wrong, Logan?"

Erin had nearly reached his side when his voice halted her in her tracks. "I don't want to hurt you!"

Drawing in a steadying breath, she asked, "Do you think you might?"

"It's possible," he muttered grimly, gazing up at the stars as if for direction. Without warning he turned, and she nearly cried out at the bleak misery in his moon bathed eyes. "I know what I feel for you is special, but I have no other comparisons to draw on. You are outside my experience, so unlike anyone else I've ever known. My upbringing has been so different from yours, Erin. I'm afraid that some day those differences will destroy what we've found together."

Logan was just telling her what she already knew. She didn't really fit into his world, but hearing him express his doubts was nevertheless a crippling blow. She should have been angry, she should have been resentful, but she couldn't blame him for voicing his uncertainties. How could she, when his tight-lipped anguish mirrored her own? Instead all she felt right then was sadness, because she was convinced that any happiness they found was doomed to be fleeting.

Yet she set such knowledge aside, determined not to sully what they had with dread of an indeterminate future. She would face the loneliness of separation from Logan when she had to, and not a second sooner. For now being with him, loving him, was worth any price she might have to one day pay. In that moment of awareness Erin crossed the final threshold into womanhood. She loved this man, and she was willing to risk everything on the slim chance that he would someday love her in return.

As she reached Logan's side there was a new confidence shining in her eyes, and she raised demanding arms to draw him close to her. With a muffled cry he surrendered to her embrace, and shuddered as she whispered, "Make love to me, Logan."

With a growl of need his mouth slanted across hers, his tongue demanding a surrender she granted eagerly. His hands shook as he slid the buttons free on her blouse and impatiently reached for the front fastening of her bra. Drawing his head back as he slid the clothing over her shoulders, his gaze devoured the full, rounded breasts exposed to his view.

She both saw and heard the swift inhalation of his breath, but it was the look on his face that enthralled her. A dark tide of color had seeped beneath his cheekbones, and his eyes seemed to burn her with possessive ardor. His strong jaw was locked with tension, and his lips were parted as the breath rasped heavily in his throat. "You are as beautiful as a dream."

If she had paused to think she might have been shocked by her boldness, but her hands seemed to have a mind of their own. With a tiny whimper of frustration she pressed her aching breasts against his chest. As she wrapped her arms around his waist, she gasped as his body hair abraded her sensitive nipples. The keening moan she uttered was trapped by his mouth, as he bent and lifted her into his arms.

When he laid her on top of his bed and started to rise, she clutched at his shoulders with desperate strength. "Don't leave me!"

Logan wanted to tear off his clothes and then remove the rest of her own, but her need for reassurance was more important than his urgency to feel her naked in his arms. Reclining beside her, he smiled at her with heart-stopping tenderness. "I couldn't even if I wanted to, don't you know that?"

The laugh she gave was rooted in a sob. "All I know is how much I want you. I feel like I'm burning up inside, and I don't know how to put out the fire. Teach me, Logan."

"With pleasure," he murmured softly.

While his lips surrounded the erratic pulse beating against her throat, his hand gently clasped the underside of her breast. His thumb slid back and forth over the small pink crest, causing it to swell and pucker as though begging for his touch. With a gasp she arched

her back, her entire body rigid as she buried her hands
in his dark hair.

"Is the fire burning hotter, love?" he asked, his
breath feathering her desire-dampened flesh as his lips
moved downward. "Shall I cool you with my
mouth?"

"Yes," she gasped, her body twisting in a frenzy of
erotic sensation. "Please..."

With a murmur of satisfaction his tongue laved her
nipple, then lifted to blow upon the moisture left behind. Again and again he repeated the process, until
Erin was quaking with a need for greater fulfillment.
With a low moan she twisted her fingers in his hair,
urging his complete possession of her breast with a
forceful tug.

Logan had no strength left to resist her unspoken
demand, and with an unintelligible cry of pleasure he
took her nipple into the warm, moist cavern of his
mouth. Rhythmically he began to suckle and probe the
rigid little bud with his tongue, his loins filling with
almost unbearable pressure as Erin's hips began to rise
and fall against him in instinctive syncopation.

His hand deserted her breast to release the snap on
her jeans, barely preventing himself from tearing the
zipper apart in his haste. Eventually the metal teeth
released the soft, silken flesh of her belly, and his
mouth deserted her breast, aching to satisfy another,
deeper hunger. Jackknifing into a sitting position, he
gripped the waistband of her jeans and panties and
pulled them over her hips.

Erin's eyes looked up at him, deep blue pools of
mingled delight and apprehension. "Easy, baby," he

whispered as he felt her tense beneath his hands. "I want to love all of you, every warm, beautiful inch."

"Logan, I . . ."

She forgot what she was going to say as her clothes dropped to the carpet and Logan rose to begin unfastening his cutoffs with quick, almost frenzied movements. Within seconds he stood before her, splendidly, gloriously naked, and all she could do was marvel at his perfection. If there was a trace of anxiety in her wide-eyed gaze, she pushed it to the back of her mind.

But Logan was too impatient to give her much of a chance to look at him. She blinked and his face swam into her line of vision, a slow, beautiful smile curving his lips as he braced his hands on either side of her. His knees nudged her thighs apart and he knelt between them. "Touch me," he demanded harshly, his deep voice resonating through her with quivering force. "Run your hands over my body, Erin."

The shyness she expected to feel never materialized. Instead she slid her hands over his chest and shoulders, and gloried in the warmth of his flesh. He stiffened above her, the muscles in his arms rigid and holding the faintest of tremors as her touch wandered lower. A muscle pulsed in his jaw as she scraped her nails over his taut stomach, which immediately hollowed in reaction as he sucked in his breath.

"Sweet heaven, don't stop now," he muttered through clenched teeth. "Please don't stop, baby!"

Totally abandoning herself to the sensual woman inside of her that this man had brought into existence, Erin gently reached for the pulsing hardness that proclaimed him male. Marveling at the silky smooth warmth that throbbed at her touch, she glanced down between their bodies as her other hand rose to aid in her exploration.

Logan's body jerked, and she returned her startled gaze to his face. "Did I hurt you?"

"It's a good hurt," he confessed with a shaken laugh. "Let me show you how good."

Replacing her hands at her sides, Logan taught her the truth of his words in a way that left her almost mindless with pleasure. While his mouth relearned the shape and texture of her breasts, his fingers began feathering through the pale, delicate down at the apex of her thighs. The sensations that ripped through her shocked her into momentary rigidity, but soon her body began to undulate with sensual enjoyment.

As his lips moved down her body, they paused to linger against the contracted muscles of her belly. "You see how sweet a pain it is?"

"Yes," she sighed in an ecstasy of realization. "Oh, Logan, I want . . . I need . . ."

His fingers plunged deeper, and when she cried out a husky chuckle rumbled against her thigh. "You want me, Erin? All of me?"

Gripping the comforter in clenched fists, she thrashed her head from side to side and groaned with the need building inside of her. She was beyond words, beyond rational thought, beyond anything but the urge to satisfy the pressure coalescing into a tumultuous flood in her straining body. But Logan had gone over the edge of restraint, and didn't wait for an answer to his question. All of his concentration was centered on his flagging self-control, only his desire not to cause her unnecessary pain preventing him from thrusting into her as he wanted to do.

Instead his penetration was gradual, sweat break-ing out on his skin every time he paused to allow her to adjust to him. Then the final barrier was reached, and with gritted teeth he surged forward to claim her as his own. He felt her recoil briefly, and then he trembled with relief when she tentatively lifted her hips to guide him deeper.

"Are you all right?" he whispered.

He was buried inside of her, afraid to move in case he caused her any more pain. His body was stretched over hers, his forearms braced beside her head to re-lieve her of some of his weight. The tips of his fingers brushed a few strands of hair from her flushed cheeks, and her eyes were closed. She was so still; so silent she frightened him. His repeated cry was urgent, uncer-tainty adding harshness to his voice. "Are you all right, sweetheart?"

Erin's lips barely moved, as she sighed, "I'm won-derful!"

"That you are," he agreed huskily. "You are won-derful, you feel wonderful, and if I don't finish this soon I'm going to wonderful myself to death."

Languidly her lashes rose, a sensual gleam in her eyes and laughter in her voice. "So who's stopping you?"

He brushed his lips back and forth over hers, and said against their softness, "That sounds like a chal-lenge."

Erin never had time to agree, because Logan chose that moment to begin rocking his hips gently. With a startled cry she wrapped her legs and her arms around him, clinging to him while unbelievable sensations wracked her small frame. As Logan felt her contract-

ing muscles tightening around him, his restraint gave
way to a savagely demanding urgency. He thrust in
her, through her, against her, until all Erin was aware
of was the heat and fire of his plunging body. Then the
world around her exploded, her only safe haven the
one she'd found in his arms.

Foaming sea water surged around Erin as she stood
to resist the pull of the tide. She was breathing rapidly from her last body-surfing attempt, which as
usual had resulted in her being rolled and tossed upon
the beach like a straggly clump of seaweed. Shading
her eyes with a dripping hand, she spotted a seal-dark
head and smiled. Logan was far more adventurous
than she, and was waiting for a more impressive wave
before he joined her.

With a contented sigh she threw her head back and
gazed up at the brilliantly blue sky. Far in the distance she could see a boat, the white sails reaching toward cottony puffs of summer clouds. Although it was
nearing six o'clock in the evening, she could feel the
hot August sun beating against her shoulders. Sunlight was reflected in sparkling jeweled prisms on the
ocean's surface, and towering cliffs protected this piece
of shoreline from the worst of the wind.

Never had a day been more beautiful, she decided
happily. Waking up with Logan snuggled against her
back had given her a wonderful sense of well-being,
especially when he informed her that they were taking
the day off and spending it together. And spend it together they had, she thought with a smile. After making slow, leisurely love they were ravenously hungry.
They showered together, and dressed hurriedly for a

trip into Monterey. There they devoured a spectacularly scrumptious brunch, and spent several hours peeking into the specialty shops along Cannery Row.

When they returned to the house they changed for the beach, both of them eager to spend the rest of the daylight enjoying the sand and sea. She had also enjoyed looking at Logan in his brief, snug white swimsuit, she remembered with an impudent grin. She had been tempted to drag him back inside the house, but had thoughtfully resisted temptation. After all, she didn't want to exhaust the poor man.

Pushing her hair off her face with both hands, she once again searched for that dark head bobbing in the water. Her eyes widened with apprehension when she noticed the size of the wave building behind him. Just when it seemed he would be buried beneath that massive wall of water, Logan's arms began to stroke powerfully as he battled the sea for supremacy. His body stiffened and his back arched, and the wave picked him up and hurtled him forward with amazing speed.

It was only when he was walking toward her with a huge smile on his face that she remembered how to breathe. Excitement still glittered in his eyes as he asked, ''Wasn't that a beaut?''

Beaut or not, for a few seconds there she'd been terrified. As a result, her voice shook with the remnants of fear. ''I thought it was going to drag you under.''

Immediately contrite, he drew her into his arms. ''You won't get rid of me that easily.''

''I never want to lose you,'' she whispered.

Erin's hands tightened around his neck as she gazed up at him with her heart in her eyes, and with a low groan he jerked her against his sea-slick body. As though begging for the contact, her nipples hardened, and she avoided his knowing glance in confusion. She could feel his inner heat against her one-piece maillot, the green-and-blue madras print boldly colorful against his golden, hair-matted chest. Grasping a handful of her wet, sun-streaked hair, he forced her head up with a gentle tug. Then his mouth captured hers in fierce demand, until both of them were trembling with the intensity of their desire.

"Let's get back to the house," he suggested hoarsely.

Peeping up at him from beneath demurely lowered lashes, she smiled with teasing provocation. "A shower would be nice."

His eyes sparked wickedly. "Among other things."

Erin pointed with mock regret. "Then we're through playing around in the surf?"

"We're through body-surfing, but we are definitely not through playing around."

With a husky chuckle Erin broke free of his arms, and called over her shoulder, "Last one home has to wash the other's back!" As she pelted across the sand Logan deliberately lagged behind, deciding this was one race he was going to lose.

Erin bent over the dishwasher in Logan's compact kitchen and placed the last plate in the holder. Before she could straighten firm, guiding hands grasped her hip bones and a drawling voice murmured, "You have the most delectable backside, sweetness."

"You've mentioned that a time or two," she responded dryly.

He pressed himself against her, and her breath caught as she felt the evidence of his stirring masculinity through the clothes they wore. It had been nearly a month since their trip to Monterey, and she still marveled at the explosive passion that flared between them at any given moment. It could be ignited by a single word or even a look across a room, and when they were in public their reaction to each other often became downright embarrassing.

Each new day was a single jewel strung on Erin's necklace of memories, and she savored each for the beauty of its existence. Happiness bubbled up inside her, and she sent an amused glance over her shoulder at Logan. "We are not going to make love on top of a dishwasher door, Logan."

His mouth tilted to a rakish angle. "Why not? We've done it everywhere else."

With a gurgle of mirth she bumped against him, and he jumped back with a grunt of surprise. "Hey, take it easy!"

Raising the dishwasher door as she straightened, she pushed the pre-wash button and turned to face him. Her hands on her hips in a mockingly arrogant stance, she said, "If you can't take the heat, get out of the kitchen."

Giving her an aggrieved look, he muttered, "You may have damaged me for life, woman."

With a sweetly demure smile, she asked, "Shall I kiss you and make it better?"

Logan's eyes kindled, and then began to flame. "That sounds good," he murmured thickly as he reached for her. "Is there anywhere else you'd like to injure me before we head upstairs?"

Linking her hands together behind his neck, Erin pressed a series of tiny kisses over his throat and the upper part of his chest exposed by the open collar of his silk shirt. "Now who sounds kinky?"

"Ahh, yes," he drawled with a reminiscent smile. "I accused you of that the day I dragged you out of the Monterey club. The way I remember it, you were going to tie me up and..." He paused, his hands tightening against her waist as her tongue began to lave the pulse throbbing against his throat. "You never did elaborate, honey. What were you going to do once you had me bound and at your mercy?"

Once Erin wouldn't have had a clue how to respond to that question, but after a month of Logan's tuition she was well prepared. With a giggle she stretched to her full height and began to whisper in his ear. He listened for a moment in fascinated silence, his chest beginning to rise and fall with increasing rapidity. Then he groaned and lifted her until her legs dangled uselessly, an expression of anticipation on his face as he carried her across the floor. The phone on the wall shrilled, and with a frustrated grimace he put her down and picked up the receiver. In a husky whisper he muttered, "Don't you dare move from this spot."

His eyes held both a threat and a heated promise as she took the opportunity to slip out of his arms. Deliberately flaunting his command with an impertinent toss of her head, she crossed the arched entry into the living room and glanced around her with appreciative eyes. Logan's home was set high in the Berkeley hills, and could boast a superb view of the Bay Area and even parts of San Francisco from big bay windows. It was fairly modern in design, with clean structural lines and tall cathedral ceilings. His choice of furniture was like him, she thought with a smile, large, comfortable, and graced with an elegant symmetry that was very pleasing to the eye.

Erin wandered toward the double doors on the far side of the room and stepped out onto a wooden deck dotted with redwood lawn furniture. Although there were other homes nearby, the thickly wooded grounds gave an illusion of privacy. Tilting her head back she inhaled deeply, enjoying the pungent scents that drifted on the evening breeze. Then she ambled toward her favorite spot, where a wooden, white-painted gazebo circled a sunken hot tub. Stepping through the opening, she seated herself on one of the padded bench seats that formed a rounded edged U inside the tiny building.

Several minutes passed before Logan's voice sounded from the darkness. "I figured I'd find you here."

Patting the seat beside her, she asked, "Was that call the one you've been expecting from Brian Dunlop in Eureka?"

Instead of joining her, Logan shook his head and walked toward the hot tub. He opened a self-lighting side panel, and immediately the water began to churn and foam. Frothy bubbles appeared on the surface, with billows of steam rising to mingle with the nippy air. After adjusting the temperature gauge to his satisfaction, he closed the panel and perched on the wide ledge which circled the hot tub.

His voice was unusually terse as he answered her question. "That was my mother on the phone. We're invited to a party tomorrow night."

Erin tensed and sent a searching glance over his
shadowed features. She wasn't deceived by the casual
tone of his voice, and her own sounded brittle and defensive as a result. "Why should I be invited, Logan?
They don't even know me."

"Yes, but thanks to Lorna's gossiping tongue my
mother already knows a great deal about you," he
stated bluntly. "Probably most of it false, which is
reason enough to attend."

His grim expression was disturbing. Something else
was bothering him, she decided, his tension almost
palpable. "What did your mother say to upset you,
Logan?"

He averted his eyes, his response almost rudely impatient. "Nothing!"

Logan heard the sharp breath Erin drew with a
feeling of futility, unable to offer her an explanation
for his behavior. He recalled his brief conversation
with his mother, and knew she was up to something.
When he had accepted her invitation for himself and
Erin, there had been a distinct note of satisfaction in
her voice when she said she was looking forward to
meeting his girlfriend. That alone had been enough to
arouse his suspicions, since his mother considered
anyone who wasn't a wealthy member of the country-
club set as being genetically inferior.

Glancing at Erin's bent head he felt as though he
was leading a lamb to the slaughter, but felt it was time
she saw beyond the rose-colored glasses she viewed
him through. He knew he had begun a course of action that could be the beginning of the end where they
were concerned, but it was something that had to be
done. Sooner or later she was going to have to see him

as a product of his upbringing, and it might as well be now.

Erin studied Logan's closed expression, and decided against further mention of his mother. Instead she continued with the subject he himself had introduced into their conversation. "You're right, Lorna certainly wouldn't say anything likely to endear me to your mother," she said, her voice subdued. "Do your parents know we're lovers?"

"In the circles they move in that would be taken for granted," he replied with caustic sarcasm. "Does it bother you to have them know about us?"

Erin nodded and kept her eyes trained on his face, trying to gauge his reaction as she asked, "Doesn't it bother you?"

Logan's laughter held a bitter inflection. "I don't give a damn."

Her response was softly blunt. "I think you do, Logan."

"I'll admit I'm not overjoyed at the prospect of introducing you to my family." He reached down and drew her into his arms, holding her so tightly against him she could hardly breathe. "I've been happier with you than I've ever been in my life before, and I don't want anything to spoil that happiness."

Because you know, my darling, that I'll never fit in with them, she thought sadly. The pain of that realization added firmness to her voice. "Then I won't go."

"You'll go if I have to carry you." With shocking swiftness he pulled the stretchy knit top she wore over her head, her distracted gasp muffled by the soft folds of material. "But why?" she finally managed to ask, trying to stay his hands as they went to work on the buttoned waistband of her shorts. "There's no earthly reason to involve your mother and father in our relationship."

Logan stripped the white shorts and panties down her legs and started to tug at his own clothing. "There is also no earthly reason to try to hide our relationship from them, Erin."

"I'm not trying to hide anything." With an exasperated scowl she stepped free of her discarded clothing, and sent a baleful glare in his direction. "You're the one who wants a casual affair, which makes meeting your parents inappropriate to say the least. I thought a mistress was supposed to stay quietly in the background of her lover's life."

"Don't talk like that," he grated angrily. "Don't make our relationship sound cheap and transitory."

Her eyebrows formed a mockingly derisive arch. "And isn't it?"

"You know it isn't!" When he lifted her up he appeared angry enough to throw her into the hot tub, but his movements were gently cautious as he lowered her into the water and hurriedly climbed in after her. His hands and mouth began to work their magic on her breasts, but she was determined not to let him evade this argument so easily. Pushing against his chest, she snapped, "You're not getting around me like this!"

"How about like this?" he murmured wickedly, sliding his hands over her buttocks and lifting her against his aroused hardness.

Logan's teeth scraped against a turgid nipple, and she moaned and yanked at his hair. "God," he gasped. "One of these days we're going to drown each other doing this."

Erin's peal of laughter ended in another moan, but she stubbornly continued to resist his attempts to distract her. But when his tongue began to lave the inside of her ear, she writhed against him in unbridled arousal. "Why are you being so difficult?" she questioned petulantly.

Logan glanced down toward her well-loved breasts and grinned. "It's my nature to be contrary, my darling."

She opened her mouth to retaliate, but he placed his fingers against her lips and shook his head. "Let's not argue anymore," he pleaded huskily. "Just make love to me, Erin. I need you so badly."

With a cry of acquiescence she melted against him, joy spiraling through her as she met and equaled his ardor. Her heart pounded out the rhythm of her desire, a message of pure sensuality flashing into her brain. She clung to him with arms made strong by passion, her kiss-swollen lips curving into a triumphant smile as he shuddered in her embrace.

"Yes," he gasped when she buried the smile against a hard male nipple. "Yes, use your tongue on me, sweetheart."

Erin began to lick at him in eager compliance, absorbing the taste and texture of his flesh with languid enjoyment. Her hands tangled in the hair spread across his chest, and he stiffened as they started to trace a downward path. Logan's tension increased as her nails scratched against his hard, flat belly, but when they trailed lower he exploded into movement.

No longer content to remain quiescent, he grasped her by the waist and lifted her onto the rim of the hot tub.

Her body was bathed in the moonlight escaping through the ceiling slats, and as he stood in front of her he stared at her voluptuous female form in dazed wonder. She was leaning back on her arms, her high, rounded breasts jutting forward as though proud of their perfection. The gentle flair of her hips seemed to be waiting for the grip of his hands and her smooth thighs for the plunging thrust of his body.

"You bewitch me," he whispered.

Erin looked back at him in near reverence. "As you do me."

With gentle insistence he parted her thighs, and slid closer until he was kneeling on the bench hidden beneath the churning water. Leaning forward, he pressed his open mouth against her arched throat. His tongue moved in a circular pattern over the pulsating cord he found there, absorbing the taste and texture of her flesh with a hungry urgency that only seemed to increase the more it was fed. The muscles on his abdomen clenched as his head wandered lower, until his teeth scraped against the yielding softness of her breast.

Erin couldn't prevent the gasping cry that escaped her, nor the way her body jerked forward to assist his exploration. Her hands gripped his cheeks as she guided his mouth to where she needed it most, shockwaves of pleasure rippling through her as his lips enclosed a turgid nipple. "Harder," she demanded as he began to suck the aching nub deeper into his mouth. "Do it harder, Logan!"

Although he complied, dividing his attention equally between both breasts, it wasn't enough for either of them. Logan's hunger to taste the very essence of her body quickly burned out of control, and with a choked exclamation he urged her to lie back against the mist-warmed wooden deck. Sensing his intention, Erin tried to hide herself from the brooding intensity of his gaze.

Shyly her hands attempted to guard the golden down which sheltered her femininity from a touch she hadn't yet allowed. Her eyes were filled with a fear of the unknown, her voice a whimper of doubtful reluctance. "No, Logan. I don't want..."

"I'll make you want," he breathed huskily. "I'll make you want until you scream with pleasure."

Before she had a chance to protest any further, Logan lifted her hands and held them against her sides. Then his mouth closed over his goal, and his growl of satisfaction blended with Erin's shocked cry. But soon shock faded, giving way to the incredible sensations bursting inside of her. Her hips rose and fell in a mindless ritual of desire, as Logan's lips and tongue became instruments of delight and torture. As he eventually devoured the convulsive flood of her passion, she was soon crying out his name in an endless litany of rapture.

Shudders still wracked her as Logan began to sweep his restless hands up and over every curve of her body, miraculously reviving her passion until she twisted beneath his touch. Propelling himself from the water in a single lunge, he bent over her supine form and smiled his satisfaction. "Thank you," he whispered tenderly. "Thank you for giving yourself to me so generously."

Erin brushed the hair from his forehead, her face flushed with becoming color. "Shouldn't I be saying that to you?"

His mouth formed a smug curve. "Do you want to?"

"Mmm," she murmured drowsily.

Logan braced his arm beside her and demandingly rubbed his painfully aroused body against her. "Don't you dare go to sleep, woman! In case you haven't noticed, I'm not finished yet."

With a gurgle of laughter she wrapped her arms around his waist, her hips seeking to deepen the contact as she drew him down to her. "And in case you haven't noticed," she replied teasingly, gripping his hips to guide him inside her welcoming warmth, "neither am I."

Ten

———

Logan parked his car along the curve of the wide, circular drive that fronted his parents' home. A string of strategically placed floodlights illuminated the house and grounds, and the sound of a band tuning up reached them on the evening breeze. He gazed impersonally through his car window at the white, three-storey mansion fronted by tall columns reminiscent of pre-Civil War southern architecture. Then he glanced toward the woman beside him, his mouth quirking wryly as he correctly interpreted her awestruck expression.

"Don't look so overwhelmed, Erin." He flung his hand outward in a dismissive gesture. "It's only a house."

"I had no idea," she murmured quietly. "I knew

you came from a prominent family, but I never expected this kind of grandeur.''

"It's all window dressing," he remarked bitterly. "Just an empty shell reflecting the emptiness of the people who live there."

Logan abruptly thrust open his door, his footsteps calmly measured as he circled the vehicle. In actuality he wanted to run; to prevent Erin from being exposed to the brittle, aimless atmosphere inside that house where he'd grown up, and to protect her from the cruel, self-centered people who inhabited a world he'd long ago turned from in revulsion.

As he helped Erin exit the car, he covered the hand she placed in the crook of his elbow with his own. They slowly mounted the wide stone steps leading to the front entrance, and he wished he could cover her eyes and ears as well. His mother and her contemporaries, not to mention the rest of his erstwhile family, could savage a sweet innocent like Erin without even trying.

Soon she would be able to comprehend the reality of his background for herself, and her romantic delusions would be shattered. After that, it wouldn't be long before she realized he wasn't the kind of man she could share her future with. Dear God, he didn't want to lose her, but she had to be made to understand how impossible it would be for them to emulate her parents' simple, uncomplicated relationship! She would see the futility of trying to share her dreams with a man who had grown up in an environment so alien to her own, but the pain of disillusion would fade in time. Heaven help him, it wouldn't ever fade for him, but it was the only way he could save her from even worse anguish in the future!

Erin had grown up protected from the tainted morality he'd been exposed to, in a home where principles such as honor and human dignity were revered and upheld. But tonight she was going to view a side of life she couldn't possibly imagine, and one to which she should never have to be exposed. It was his fault she was going to be subjected to the kind of people who had reduced cruel maliciousness to a fine art, and the thought sickened him.

With this in mind he turned to her, a deep frown scoring lines beside his mouth. "Stay close to me, Erin. I don't want you wandering around on your own."

Mistakenly thinking him concerned with her making some dreadful faux pas if he wasn't there to prevent it, Erin rounded on him indignantly. "You don't have to worry. I'm not going to embarrass you, Logan."

"No," he ground out harshly, "but the actions of some of my mother's less-esteemed guests might embarrass you, sweetheart. If this party runs true to form, in a couple of hours half the men will be as high as kites and looking for a little feminine company to take upstairs. Do you get the picture?"

Erin hoped she didn't look as shocked by his offensive disclosure as she felt, but could see by the shrewd comprehension in his eyes that her wishes were in vain. But accompanying his knowing expression was the pain her words had caused him, and her features crumpled in remorse. "I'm sorry for snapping at you like that, but I'm so nervous I feel like screaming. I didn't mean what I said, Logan."

His face grew pale as he held her gaze, his voice filled with anguished regret as he muttered, "Jesus, it's starting already."

Confused by the cryptic comment, she asked, "What's starting? You're not making any sense, Logan."

Logan didn't bother to respond, instead leading her past the uniformed maid who opened the door to them with a politely murmured greeting. Nodding his head with formal courtesy, he asked stiltedly, "Are my parents in the ballroom, Eloise?"

"No, sir, they're waiting for you in the library," the woman replied just as formally. "They wish to speak with you before the majority of the guests arrive."

As the maid hurried off, Logan followed her retreating figure with a cryptic gaze. "I'll just bet they do."

Erin stared at him in consternation, unable to believe the change that had come over him since they had entered his parents' estate. He was dour and taciturn, and inexplicably defensive. With a worried frown, she whispered, "Logan, why are you so angry? I thought you wanted to come here tonight."

His chest expanded as he filled his lungs with a calming breath, his features carefully controlled as he attempted a tight-lipped smile. "If I had my way I'd never enter this cursed mausoleum again. God, but I hated this place as a boy!"

Erin's concern deepened as she acknowledged the pain beneath his surly behavior. Lifting a caressing hand to his cheek, she whispered, "Are the memories that terrible, darling?"

Logan didn't have to reply, because the answer was there in his darkly brooding eyes. With a murmur of compassion, she placed a kiss against the corner of his mouth. "I wish I could replace all the bad memories with good ones," she said softly.

He bent to place his mouth against her forehead, his voice muffled against her skin. "Sweet, gentle little love. What will I do without you?"

Erin was suddenly frightened by his inexplicable behavior, her heart sensing the bewildering turmoil he was experiencing. "Since I have no intention of leaving you, you won't have to do without me. Why would you make a remark like that?"

Once again he refused to answer, removing her hand from his arm so he could link her fingers through his. Then he pulled her toward a wide, curving staircase that opened onto a long gallery. Plush carpeting muffled their footsteps as they climbed to the second floor and crossed to stand in front of a pair of elaborately carved double doors. Logan knocked briefly and released her hand to push the doors inward, and Erin couldn't suppress a gasp at the dimensions of the room into which he led her.

Every inch of wall space from floor to ceiling was covered with bookshelves. Two crystal chandeliers, each easily as wide as her Volkswagen bug was long, hung suspended from a twenty-foot ceiling edged in gilt. A white marble fireplace was flanked on either side by towering mullioned windows, and twin oriental vases of immense proportions graced either side of the hearth. A handsome walnut desk was situated in one corner, while a white velvet modular sofa unit took up space along the opposite wall.

Erin glanced in that direction, her eyes widening apprehensively. She had expected Logan's mother and father to be present, but wasn't prepared for the other people who watched their approach with a curiously avid intensity. Glancing up at Logan in confusion, her stomach began to churn as she noticed the unguarded revulsion in his eyes. "Logan, what's going on?" she questioned nervously. "Who are all these people?"

His lip curled in disgust. "You see before you the entire Sinclair ménage, minus a couple of younger cousins. As I suspected, my mother has outdone herself this time."

A stout, gray-haired man rose to his feet and walked toward them, his hand held out in greeting. "Logan," he said as he shook hands and turned toward Erin with a rather ineffectual smile. "Won't you introduce me to your friend?"

"This is Erin Daniels, Father." Erin glanced from the elderly man to Logan, appalled by the stiffly correct behavior of father and son. They could have been two strangers discussing the weather for all the warmth there was between them. "Erin, my father, James Sinclair."

Her own father would have immediately put a guest at ease by suggesting the use of his first name, but James Sinclair merely nodded and guided them toward a tall, elegantly garbed matron who was holding court at the far end of the room. She noticed that Logan had inherited her dark hair and green eyes, but there any similarity ended. The older woman's mouth was etched into permanent lines of discontent, her smile as cold as Logan's was warm. At her side stood Lorna Phelps, and Erin's heart smote her at the combined hostility emanating from the two women.

A pair of chillingly antagonistic eyes slid contemptuously over her son and his companion, her thin, pointed chin held at an imperious angle. "You're late, Logan! I distinctly remember telling you we expected your arrival in advance of our other guests so Ms. Daniels could be properly acknowledged."

With deceptive nonchalance Logan glanced at his watch, then returned his mocking gaze to his mother's disapproving countenance. "How clever of you to notice, Mother."

Erin gaped at him in surprise, unused to hearing such a sarcastic inflection in his voice. This rude, caustic individual wasn't the tender, kind man she loved. She was seeing a cold, ruthless side to Logan's personality she'd never known existed, and she was shocked by the change in him. There was bewilderment in her eyes as she looked at him; a febrile glitter in his as he gave her a reckless smile in return.

"Erin, I'd like you to meet my mother, Gladys Sinclair. Mother, this is Erin Daniels ... my fiancée."

Erin's startled gasp was concealed by Lorna Phelps's scream of outrage. Automatically she turned her attention to the other woman, shivering with revulsion at the loathing in those black, reptilian eyes. In a strident voice which carried easily to every corner of the room, Lorna sneered, "You were more clever than I thought, you little whore. Not content with sharing Logan's bed, you manipulated him into offering you respectability. Just how far along are you, darling?"

Erin went white, the blood leaving her stricken face in a rush. "How dare you!"

Lorna lunged forward, fingers curled like claws as she screeched, "I'll dare, you sneaky..."

Before those raking nails could connect with Erin's tender flesh, merciless hands gripped Lorna's wrists. "That's enough," Logan muttered in disgust as he flung her away from him. "You will apologize to Erin this instant, Lorna."

Gladys Sinclair stepped forward and placed a protective arm around her goddaughter's waist, her voice filled with derision as she surveyed Erin's trembling body. "Why should she apologize for the truth, Logan? This impudent little hayseed has made a fool of you, but my eyes aren't blinded by lust."

Logan drew Erin against his side. "You're too selfish and filled with deceit to recognize the truth."

"I know this much," she countered chillingly. "If you persist with this folly you will be disinherited!"

"You must realize by now that I'm impervious to your threats. I'll marry whomever I damn well please."

"You don't honestly think a person like this will be accepted into the family, do you?"

"I don't give a damn if Erin is ever acknowledged by this pack of jackals, Mother."

An angry murmur of voices greeted his words, and Erin flinched as contemptuous, outraged eyes took delight in her humiliation. Where before she'd been pale, her face was now burning with humiliation. Yet she didn't try to use Logan as a buffer, her body cringing in rejection as she pulled away from him. Her mind replayed the lie he'd told his mother, and she wanted to scream with pain at his betrayal.

How could he have used a nonexistent engagement between them to deliberately precipitate this nasty scene? she wondered sickly. He must have known how his family would react to such a disclosure, and yet he had thrown her into this pit of vipers without the least compunction. He was using her to score off his mother, and a barely banked rage grew inside of her at the thought.

Straightening her spine, she escaped the warmth of Logan's body and surveyed him with accusing eyes. "You'll have my resignation on your desk Monday morning."

"Erin, I..."

Ignoring him, she turned with touching dignity toward his mother. "You needn't worry, Mrs. Sinclair. I have no intention of marrying into your family. You see, I'm rather choosey in the company I keep."

Lorna's fury erupted into the incredulous silence which resulted from Erin's taunt. "Are you going to let her talk to your mother like that, Logan?"

He responded with a derisive grin. "If Mother can dish it out, she can take it, Lorna."

"You shut up," Erin rounded on him furiously. "I don't need to be championed by a man too cowardly to tell me we were through to my face." She shook her head, anguish clouding her eyes. "Oh, Logan, you didn't have to use this underhanded method to make me realize our relationship was over. A simple good-bye would have sufficed."

He whitened at the accusation, his features convulsing in despair. "You've got it all wrong, Erin. It was never my intention to end our relationship, and especially not like this. I only wanted you to realize..."

"You only wanted me to realize that I'd never be welcomed by your family," she interrupted coolly. She surveyed the other occupants of the room with visible disgust, her hands clenching at her sides as she struggled to suppress the tears clogging her throat. "Well, your ingenious ploy worked. I wouldn't marry into this vicious, unprincipled bunch if my life depended on it!"

The laugh she uttered held unmistakable bitterness and scorn as she returned her gaze to Logan's tense features. "And to think that I once thought myself unworthy of your love; too far down on the social scale to aspire to such heights. But I don't feel like that any longer, Logan. If I've learned one lesson tonight, it's that you and your illustrious family are the ones unworthy of me."

Logan recoiled as though struck. His whisper held only hollow emptiness, but there was bitter regret in his eyes. "I know, sweetheart."

The endearment succeeded in shattering Erin's flagging control. With an aggrieved cry she began running, her only thought to escape from the pain ripping her apart inside. Tears poured down her face as she wrenched open the library doors and tore down the stairs. She passed the maid Eloise in the entry. As she caught sight of the young woman's startled expression, she nearly gave in to an hysterical urge to laugh. She knew she must look like a wild woman, but she was beyond caring about making a good impression. She was beyond caring about anything!

As she escaped into the night Erin heard Logan's voice calling her name, but she ignored the frantic summons. Stumbling and weaving, she reached an opening in the dense thicket of trees which surrounded the Sinclair estate. Ignoring the branches and brambles that tore at her flimsily covered flesh, sobs wrenched her body as she disappeared into the forested shadows. If shielding herself from the crippling blow she'd just been dealt meant braving the unknown darkness, she would do so gladly.

Anything was better than facing the lover who no longer wanted her in his life.

"Erin, for God's sake answer me!"

Too exhausted to move, Erin heard the thud of footsteps drawing close to her with a sense of hopelessness. She was sitting upon a soft carpet of moss, her head resting against the trunk of an old, gnarl-limbed oak. From the sounds Logan was making as he tore through the concealing greenery, she knew there was no longer any point in remaining silent. In another few minutes he'd be stumbling over her anyway, so she might as well assist the inevitable. Closing her eyes, she responded to his call. "I'm over here, Logan."

Within seconds a wild-eyed man burst into the small clearing, his frantic glance taking in the apathetic figure before him. The scratches on Erin's arms and legs were revealed by the moonlight, her gold chiffon dress torn and her panty hose shredded. She appeared heartbreakingly fragile as she lifted wounded eyes to his face, and her expression was hauntingly vulnerable as she watched his approach.

Logan shuddered visibly, his throat constricted with emotion. His chest rose and fell as he gazed at her hungrily, panic subsiding into a relief so great he swallowed past the threatening tears. She reminded him of a porcelain figurine, a dainty shepherdess who would shatter into a thousand pieces at the touch of a careless hand. But now that the damage was done, he realized that Erin's appearance was deceptive. Her loving nature gave her a strength which would never allow her to be broken, especially by a family such as his.

He should have trusted in her ability to withstand their opposition, just as he should have trusted her with his heart. All of his life he had fought his mother's ruthless domination, determined not to give in and become a broken facsimile of a man as his father had. He had viewed his parents' marriage as a battle for supremacy, instead of the partnership it should have been. Love had kept his father a prisoner of his own emotions, and he'd vowed never to be caught in a similar trap. But now he realized that the kind of love his father felt for his mother in no way resembled his own for Erin. It was a sick obsession, and not the thing of beauty Erin had showed him love could be.

Erin's developing self-confidence had never been a threat to his masculine pride, and never could be. She possessed an intrinsic strength that forebore playing games with a man's emotions. She had the courage of her convictions, and a sweetness of spirit which only sought to nurture and protect. While his mother and others like her were weak, selfish individuals without warmth or compassion, who were to be pitied instead of feared.

The realization freed something inside of him, and as he looked at Erin he felt himself begin to dream. She had done that for him, by reaching past his fears and insecurities to give him hope for a future rich with promise. Instead of showing him the ugliness of reality, she had shown him the glorious simplicity of love. Now it was up to him to convince her of all he had learned.

Moving forward at a leisurely pace, he whispered, "Your lovely dress is ruined."

"Go away," she responded sullenly. "I was sitting here praying I'd never have to see you again."

"I don't blame you," he acknowledged. "I'm not too fond of myself at the moment, either."

Erin hunched her shoulders and wrapped her arms around her raised knees, keeping her eyes averted. "You set me up tonight, Logan."

"In a way I suppose that's true, but not for the reason you think."

Logan lowered himself to the ground beside her and sighed heavily. "I don't deserve someone like you, and you had to see why for yourself."

Cautiously Erin turned her head to look at him, her confusion obvious. "But you used a phony engagement between us to humiliate me, so I'd realize I had no place in your life."

"In my heart our engagement is as real as my love for you, Erin."

"You love me?" she whispered. "Then why?"

"Because I knew that eventually you'd have to meet my parents, and once you did I figured you would be so disgusted with them you'd leave me. When you spoke of your own parents it was with so much love and pride, I was ashamed and afraid for you to meet mine. For as long as I can remember I've been ashamed of what they represent, Erin.''

She frowned at him. ''But why would you be afraid?''

''Because I didn't think you'd want to marry a man with my kind of background.''

''That's why you wanted to give me time to get to know you before we became lovers,'' she whispered incredulously. ''You thought I'd discover some flaw in you and back away. That's also why you were so certain you'd hurt me, because you're afraid that some day you'll turn out like your mother and father.''

''Can you blame me?'' he retorted savagely. ''They provided me with my example of adulthood, and children subconsciously emulate their parents. I felt you'd be better off without me in your life. I wasn't taking any chances with your happiness.''

''Oh, Logan!'' She laid her hands against his chest and gazed at him with troubled eyes. ''If only you'd trusted me enough to explain the way you felt!''

Tears filmed Erin's eyes, this time for the joy bursting for release inside of her. ''You stupid big oaf, I could shake you until your bones rattle. I thought I was lacking in confidence, but you're the real master of the art of self-delusion. Don't you realize how unique you are? You were strong enough to form your own values and to set your own goals in life, and are not and never could be a clone of your parents. You are Logan Sinclair, the man I love and respect more than anyone else in the world.''

Erin threw her arms around his neck, a huge grin spreading across her face. ''Loving me is going to cost you, mister. In case you've forgotten, you've been disinherited."

Pulling her down onto the sweet-smelling moss, Logan leaned over her with a devilish smile of his own. "Will you mind marrying a poor man, little mouse?"

"Not a bit," she retorted cheerfully. "Just an occasional piece of cheese and you are all I'll need to be happy."

"I think I can manage that." He kissed the tip of her nose, his eyes alight with adoration. "I am not dependent on my parents for any kind of financial support, Erin. What I have I've worked for, and inherited wealth means nothing to me. You are all that matters, you and the children we'll someday share. You're my life, Erin."

She began running her fingers through his hair, a dreamy smile curving her mouth. "I'll always love you, Logan."

"That's all I ask," he murmured hoarsely. "Just love me and don't ever stop."

*   *   *   *   *

SILHOUETTE® Desire™

COMING NEXT MONTH

#577 CANDLELIGHT FOR TWO—Annette Broadrick
Steve Donovan was the last person Jessica Sheldon wanted to accompany
her to Australia. Can two people who've made fighting into an art find
forever in each other's arms?

#578 NOT EASY—Lass Small
Detective Winslow Homer thought finding Penelope Rutherford's missing
camera would be a snap. But it wasn't so easy—and neither was getting
Penelope to admit that she found him irresistible!

#579 ECHOES FROM THE HEART—Kelly Jamison
Brenna McShane had never forgotten her very sexy—and very
unreliable—ex-husband. Then Luke McShane returned, bringing
home all the remembered pain . . . and all the remembered passion of
their young love.

#580 YANKEE LOVER—Beverly Barton
Historian Laurel Drew was writing her ancestor's biography when
unrefined John Mason showed up with a different story. Soon sparks were
flying between this Southern belle and her Yankee lover.

#581 BETWEEN FRIENDS—Candace Spencer
When reasonable Logan Fletcher proposed marriage to his best friend,
Catherine Parrish, it wasn't for love. Could he ever understand
Catherine's utterly romantic reasons for accepting?

#582 HOTSHOT—Kathleen Korbel
July's *Man of the Month*, photojournalist Devon Kane liked to be where
the action was. But with his latest subject—reclusive Libby Matthews—
Devon found the greatest adventure was love!

AVAILABLE NOW:

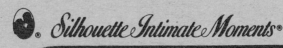

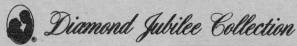